Thank.
Science Fictio.  ...ia

James Flynn

James Flynn grew up in Kent, England.

He's taken on many different roles in his life so far: juvenile delinquent, car paint sprayer, soldier in the British Army, twenty-something delinquent, graffiti artist, lorry driver, part-time portrait painter, English teacher and, of course, author.

His ultimate dream as an author is to cause a reader to be confined to a mental institution and sectioned under the mental health act after reading one of his stories, although he admits that this is a bit optimistic.

James's work has appeared in *Black Petals Magazine*, *Yellow Mama Magazine*, *The Scare Room Podcast*, *Weird Mask Magazine*, *Sugar Spice Erotica Review*, *Patty's Short Stax Anthology*, *Local Haunts Anthology* and *Lurking in the Dark Anthology*.

For your post-internet brain

ACKNOWLEDGEMENTS

I would like to thank A. Cheley, Sarah Miller, Erik McGowan and Michelle Currie for beta reading the early draft of this story. Your feedback is valued and appreciated.

I would also like to thank Lezlie Smith from The Nerdy Narrative YouTube channel for raising awareness of the book. It's always an honour to see my work on your channel.

I would like to thank my cover designer, Alison Litchfield, for creating a great cover for the book. I would like to thank my editor, Vince Fibbins, for your diligence and attention to detail. And, grudgingly, I would like to thank social media. Without you, I suppose this book would never have been written.

PREFACE

As a writer, I am naturally drawn towards anything disturbing. Unlike many other writers, though, I tend to avoid supernatural elements. In my opinion, the real world is the most disturbing place of all.

I'm old enough to remember the world as it was before smartphones and social media. For this reason, I am able to recognise, quite clearly, what the smartphone/social media phenomenon really is: a pandemic. Not only do people use their smartphones whilst eating, drinking, walking, driving, and standing at urinals (yes, I have seen people doing this), they are also willing to upload their intimate private lives to these money-making social media platforms—this is not supernatural, this is the real world.

Thanks for the Memory explores a possible consequence of this social media craze. Whilst reading this book, it is my hope that you will gradually be able to recognise how bizarre the relationship between humans and technology is becoming, but above all else, it would be nice to see you have some kind of nightmare or nervous breakdown by the time you finish it.

Hey, don't be angry at me. Look on the bright side: if you need emergency psychiatric treatment, it will give you something to tweet about. Tragic posts tend to get the most likes and shares, after all.

Reed Blagden is his name
He likes to tell rude jokes
The gags have gained him fame
With lowly drunken folks
One night at home, alone
Relaxing in his flat
He tapped his shiny phone
And opened up an app
The app was NeuroStar
With wires for your brain
It really is quite smart
But frightful, all the same
Old Reed, he sure was game
He gave the app a try
At first, it all seemed lame
Until he felt the pain

Thanks for dropping by. My name's Reed. Reed Blagden, to be precise. I'm the one who's going to be telling you this messed-up story. Now, before we start, I'd just like to get a few things straight. Unlike some narrators, I've got absolutely no problem when it comes to breaking the fourth wall and speaking directly to you. There will be no separation between the two of us during this peculiar tale, it will be as though we're sitting next to each other in some bar, chatting about the series of events like two pals. It's going to be pretty meta, believe me. No, seriously, believe me. I am looking at you right now as you read these words, and if I really wanted to I could reach out from the page and shake your hand.

Luckily for you, I have no desire to do that. It's not because I'm unfriendly, don't get me wrong; on the contrary. Most people I meet seem to think I'm friendly enough. Some people even go as far as describing me as chirpy or cheeky, but when they say that they've usually just finished watching me tell jokes up on stage.

Where was I? Oh, yes: meta, fourth wall, all that business. I will say what I want to say, and mention what I want to mention, and that includes referencing the book that you're holding in your hands right now. Don't believe me? OK, I'll do it right now: the book you're holding in your hands is called *Thanks for the Memory*. You see? I can do that. Hell, I can even go one step further and mention the name of the author, if you like, just so you can see how gutsy I am. I will directly mention the name of that irritating, red-haired, cherub-looking twat of an author called James Flynn.

You can probably sense a little bit of animosity there. Yeah, I won't deny it. I think he's a prick. Why? Well, he's responsible for putting me in this messed-up story. Or *trapping* me in this messed up story, should I say. He created me with his pen and his keyboard, brought me into being with his mind, and now I'm stuck here like a pathetic slave, destined to narrate this story over and over again for anyone who's stupid enough to buy this bloody book. I mean, if he'd made the story third person it wouldn't have been so bad. I could've just acted out the scenes, there would've been no need for me to get involved with you, the reader. But no, Mr James Flynn, Mr Look at Me I Can Write a Book Aren't I Great, had to go and make this story a first-person thing, giving me extra work to do. I think he's an asshole, I think he's an inconsiderate asshole, and I think he will always be an asshole. Furthermore, if you happen to bump into this tosser on the street, James Flynn the cretin, I urge you to verbally abuse him or, better still, physically attack him in some vicious way.

That was a bit of an aggressive start, wasn't it? I probably haven't made a very good impression. Let me put you at ease. I am actually a nice guy, I really am. And I think you'll probably warm to me by the end of the story. Maybe. Whatever happens, I'll try my best to be as bright and perky as possible for you. How about that? I can see you're not a bad person. You just want something good to read. There's nothing wrong with that.

I live in Mapharno City. You may have heard of it before, you may not have. In case you haven't, it's a wild place where strange things happen. It has skyscrapers higher than your local junkie, back alleys dirtier than your local floozy, neon lights brighter than your local rocket scientist, and roads busier than your...oh, you get the idea. It's an insane city, that's what I'm trying to say. If you want anything at all, you can find it here:

counterfeit clothes, fake jewellery, drugs, women, blah, blah, blah. Corruption is rife among the suits in government, the streets are awash with two-bob plastic gangsters, and you can't swing a dead cat downtown without it hitting some kind of hustler. Are you getting the picture now? Mapharno City is a zoo, a human zoo, and I'm just another exhibit doing my best to stay afloat and get by.

Mapharno City is both safe and unsafe at the same time. It's unsafe in the sense that anything can happen and you never know what's lurking around the corner, but it's also safe in the sense that if you keep your head down and try to live an honest life, you can probably do so and remain unscathed.

Do I keep my head down, I hear you ask? Well, I have a bit of a surprise for you here. Would you believe me if I told you that I'm a celebrity? Would you believe me if I told you that I, Mr Reed Blagden, am famous? Hey, stop laughing! I'm not joking! Well, that's not entirely true. That's basically the reason I'm famous. I'm a well-known comedian on the Mapharno City stand-up comedy circuit. I've been on TV, I've performed at huge venues, and I've had people asking me for autographs outside clubs. Shocking, eh? I'll give you a minute to digest this information before I continue. It's quite a bombshell, I realise that.

Now, as an honest man, I will admit that my level of fame has dropped a little over the years; my name doesn't create the buzz that it used to. However, it's still fair to say that I'm something of a household name. People of a certain age recognize me on the street, people involved in certain scenes recognize my billboard posters, and I still get fairly regular work. OK, sure, I don't get big arena bookings anymore, but

I still perform at least once a week. Sleazy, backstreet bars usually, if the truth be told, but it's still work, isn't it? You know the cheap-looking watering holes you see down alleyways in dodgy areas? The ones with flickering neon signs and punters vomiting outside on the doorstep? That's where my money comes from. I tell sleazy jokes in even sleazier bars to scrape a living. Comedy is a ruthless business, you know. It's a serious business, too, ironically. I'm not even forty years old, and it sometimes seems as though the industry has used me and spat me out already.

Hey, take that sad look off your face! I'm not getting the violin out here, or anything like that. My career hasn't completely gone down the pan. As I say, a lot of people still know who I am and...well, I just need to get myself back up to where I was before, I suppose.

Moreover, being a comedian at any level has its perks. For example, I get to meet all kinds of interesting characters. Working in these bars and clubs over the years, I've met countless musicians, singers, drummers, guitarists, pianists, you name it. Stage acts, as well. When I say stage acts, I mainly mean magicians. You tend to see magicians in the slightly more upmarket places, but they're certainly no strangers to the sleazy places, either. Believe me, I've seen more rabbits being pulled out of hats than the great Houdini himself, I've seen more card tricks than a Las Vegas casino veteran, and I'm more familiar with smoke and mirrors than a career politician.

Who else do I encounter during my working nights? Let me see...dancers, yeah, that's it. I see lots of dancers. Flamenco dancers, pole dancers, all that stuff. I meet hypnotists now and again, too. They're a funny bunch, I tell you. And when I say funny, I mean weird. They get people up on stage, eating onions like they're apples, and all that malarkey. It's clever, really, what they do. I consider it to be a form of psychology. Manipulative psychology, sure, but psychology nonetheless. And then, of course, there are the punters. The drinkers, the drunks, the backstreet locals, the lowlifes, the women, the bartenders, the outcasts, the crooks, and...well, look, I'm getting ahead of myself here. You'll find out about this stuff in due course. You wait and see.

* * *

The story. You want to get into the nuts and bolts of the story, right? Of course you do. Well, the first thing I need to make clear is that the residents of Mapharno City are completely hooked on social media, just like everybody else these days. Glued to their phones, the lot of them. I see it everyday, and it annoys the hell out of me. People looking at their screens whilst walking along the pavement. Tap, tap, tap, scroll, scroll, scroll. People looking at their screens whilst driving. Tap, tap, tap, scroll, scroll, scroll. People looking at their screens whilst paying for things in shops. Tap, tap, tap, scroll, scroll, scroll. You know what? I bet a lot of them tap and scroll whilst taking a dump. In fact, the other day I walked into the toilet in a bar I was performing at, and saw somebody looking at their smartphone whilst pissing into a urinal! Whilst taking a piss! Can you believe that? Can people not even take a two-minute breather from their screens to urinate? Bloody hell, it wouldn't surprise me if some of them look at their screens whilst on the job with their wives. Pump, pump, pump, tap, tap, tap, scroll, scroll, scroll. Anyway, I digress.

Mapharno City is full of these phone addicts, these screen junkies, and so when a new social media app arrived on the scene a little while back, everyone lapped it up. It revolutionised the world of social media overnight, and took things to a whole new level. This app goes by the name of NeuroStar, and it differs from all the others in the way that it gives users the ability to upload memories onto the site and share them with the world. That doesn't sound very revolutionary when you first hear it, does it? I mean, everybody uploads memories onto social media, right? Holiday snaps, and that? Well, I'm not talking about that. No, no, no, this is different. NeuroStar takes things one step further, you see, and literally allows users to upload memories. I'm talking straight from the brain, baby. Memories straight from the grey matter. Don't ask me how they managed to develop this thing, as I'm not really a tech person. I use tech, sure, but I'm old enough to have been raised in the pre-internet era, and so I'm not as tech-savvy as some of these teenage screeners.

Despite being new on the scene, the NeuroStar Corporation received some bad press very quickly, so I resisted downloading the app to my own phone for a while. I don't know the ins and outs of the whole story, but apparently, the CEO of the whole enterprise is a bit of a shady fucker. He's one of those big-time businessmen, you know? Millions in the bank, fierce attitude, takes no shit from anyone, chequered past, all that malarky. That's what I heard, anyway. The press was going on about him for a while after the app hit the market. A history of violent behaviour, one news reporter said, if my memory serves me correctly. That's the kind of picture they painted of him.

Anyway, I can tell you that if you want to upload a memory onto the NeuroStar platform, you need to do two things: 1. Download the app to your device. 2. Purchase a set of Neurodes from one of the main retailers. What are Neurodes, I hear you ask? They're part of the NeuroStar package, basically a commercialised, portable, plug-in set of electrodes that stick to your head. The kind of thing you see scientists use on TV when they read people's brainwaves, and all that stuff. Those sticky patches and wires that make people look like a futuristic Medusa, or something. The NeuroStar Corporation created these affordable packs of electrodes that people can carry around with them, and stick to their heads. Pretty neat, eh? Well, not really. As you're about to find out.

It was late at night, and I was sitting in my apartment. This was like, I don't know, about eighteen months ago now. I was a bit tipsy after drinking two or three beers after a tough gig. I bombed pretty hard in this shithole joint over in District 3, told a few clangers that didn't get any laughs, and I suppose I had to drown my sorrows as soon as I got off the damn stage. What was that joke I told? The one that got zero laughs? Oh, yeah, that's it: Did you hear about the dyslexic pimp? He bought a warehouse! I mean, come on! That's a pretty good joke, but it was met with a wall of silence that night. Stand-up comedy is unpredictable like that. Different crowds, different venues, different moods and atmospheres, you never know what punters are going to think of your material. Anyway, my act bombed in this club, and I was sitting indoors later that night in a state of slight inebriation. I was trying to decide whether to have one more beer from my mini-fridge or call it a night and go to bed, when I glanced over at this shelving rack I have on my wall. It was then that I remembered, dear reader, that I'd gone out and bought a set of these stupid Neurodes a few days before. There they were, sitting on one of the shelves, still in the plastic packaging.

I know what you're thinking. You're thinking that I'm a hypocrite, right? A moment ago, I was complaining about people who use social media apps, and here I am now telling you that I'd bought a set of NeuroStar Neurodes. Look, don't get me wrong here, of course I use social media a little bit. It's almost impossible not to nowadays, isn't it? But I'm not one of these screen zombies who use apps whilst walking down the street and taking a piss, that's for sure. So, yes, I purchased the Neurodes. And, yes, I also downloaded the app to my phone. But cut me a little bit of slack, will you?

Besides, there was actually a cunning plan behind my purchase. Remember earlier on, when I said that I need to get myself back up to where I was before? To reignite my fame? Well, when this app began to take off, I saw an opportunity. I saw an opportunity to market myself on this thing in a unique way, an opportunity to upload some comedic material, to reach out and remind people of what I'm capable of. There was method in my madness, in other words.

So there I was, in my apartment. I took these Neurodes down from the shelf, and opened them. The NeuroStar app was already installed on my phone at this point, as I said, and my "Comedian Reed Blagden" profile was all set up, so I decided that this was the time for my first memory upload. Before I started sticking the pads to my head, though, I had to think of something funny to upload. What memory did I have stored in my head that would get people laughing? Or, at the very least, what memory did I have that would shock people? My main aim at this point was to get my name circulating again, so shock value could substitute comedic value if need be. This is the beauty of being a comedian, you see. You don't have to worry so much about keeping a squeaky-clean image; in fact, if your image is too clean and innocent, it can work against you.

Memories, memories, memories. I was racking my brain for funny memories, dear reader, and I was racking it hard. Lewd memories, outrageous memories, sordid memories, any damn memory at all that would shine a spotlight on me. After ten minutes or so of dithering and fretting, it hit me; it hit me like a bolt from the blue. This saucy memory popped up onto the surface of my brain, rising into my mind like a dislodged bubble from a deep seabed. A grin spread across my stubbled jaw as I contemplated it. *This is the one*, I thought. *This is the one, indeed.*

Remember I told you earlier on that I meet a lot of people whilst working in bars? Well, I think I also mentioned that I meet a lot of women, too. Not always, don't get me wrong, I'm not going to try and paint myself as some kind of Casanova here, but now and again it happens. And so, as I was trying to think of a good memory to upload, I remembered this night where I performed in a shady little place called Bar 5. It's in District 5, hence the name, and it's a rotten venue. I put on a great show on the night in question, though, and I told some beautiful one-liners. The audience seemed to like me straight away. Maybe it was because they were all off their tits on wine, sprits and amphetamines, I don't know, but they certainly warmed to me. Hell, even my cheap, emergency gags got plenty of laughs that night, including this one: What do pussies have in common with the mafia? One slip of the tongue, and you're in deep shit.

It's like that sometimes, you know. Not the mafia, I mean performing in clubs. Sometimes the venue is right, the audience is right, the atmosphere is right, you're in the right mood, and everything just...works.

So there I was, cracking jokes on stage and lapping up the laughter, when I noticed two women sitting in the front row. They were about thirtyish from what I could see, looking up at me through plumes of cigarette smoke. They weren't stunning, I won't exaggerate here, but they were pretty damn sexy in a kind of "woman next door" way. They were giggling to each other and looking my way with glints in their eyes, there was no doubt about it. Giving off signals, you know? Playing with their hair and fluttering their eyelashes, all that seductive body language stuff. This kind of thing happens a lot, of course, people giggling and pointing, but this was different. These girls were after something, and old Reed Blagden over here knew exactly what it was!

After the gig was over, I headed over to the bar to grab a drink. Bar 5 has these wooden stools positioned around a circular bar, and I was sat on one of these trying to look cool and composed, but at the same time bobbing my head this way and that, trying to locate these two beauties. It can get quite dingy in Bar 5, and you can't really see much further than about two metres from where you're sitting due to the smoke and sweat. For a few minutes, I thought they might've left or disappeared, but, low and behold, after I'd downed a few hefty gulps of my beer, the two of them appeared out of the murk like a couple of erotic apparitions, and came striding up to me with silly smirks on their powdered faces.

Up close, I could tell that one of them was quite a bit older than the other, and it was the older one that spoke first:

'We liked your act. Very funny.'

'Thank you very much,' I replied, trying to put on my witty, handsome, nonchalant expression. 'I'm Reed. What're your names?'

Now, I felt a bit silly saying this because my name was plastered all over the walls of Bar 5 that night, and they surely must've known what my name was. But it's a kind of routine thing to say, isn't it? I think I can be forgiven for that.

'I'm Melinda,' said the older one.

'I'm Kat,' said the younger one.

'Nice to meet you, girls,' I smiled.

'I saw you on TV once,' said Melinda, with a look on her face that could've been star-struck admiration.

'Oh, yeah? When was that?'

'A couple of years back. Channel 7, I think. You were performing in a big arena.'

'I think that might've been the Comedy Convention gig,' I said, still playing it cool.

A couple of seconds then passed with both of them staring at me, and it dawned on me that they thought I was some kind of huge celebrity star, or something. *Opportunity knocks*, I thought. It was time to take control of the situation, and strike while the iron was hot.

'Would you like a drink?' I asked them both.

And so, dear reader, just like that, we got chatting. Then the chatting turned to flirting. Personal space was reduced, and the touching of hands and brushing of shoulders was increased. It was getting a bit steamy at one point, I kid you not. People were beginning to stare; we were actually causing a scene.

Knocking back the last mouthful of my drink, I turned to them and said, 'Hey, girls, how do you fancy heading over to the Majestic bar with me? It's getting a bit crowded in here.'

This was a bit of a crafty move on my part, because the Majestic is actually the name of a hotel. It was a subtle way of saying, "Do you want to go to a hotel with me?" You have to play these things clever, though, don't you?

After a brief glance at each other, they replied in unison, 'Yeah, OK.'

We walked out of the club, all three of us together, and hailed a taxi. My thoughts consisted of one thing at this point: *game on!*

At this point in the story, dear reader, I am faced with a slight predicament. I am very aware that you may be the kind of person who would like to hear about everything that happened between me and the two girls that night, with no sordid detail left out. You may be the sort of reader who likes a bit of smut, a bit of literary sleaze, or a bit of linguistic hanky-panky. However, on the other hand, you may be the kind of reader who turns their nose up at such a thing. You may be the kind of reader who would rather I skim over the steamy, explicit details of my threesome encounter.

So, what do I do? Which approach should I take? Should I be a coward and hold back the details, for fear of upsetting you? Or should I be brazen, and hit you with it full force? It's a tough one, it really is. OK, look, here's what I'm going to do. I'm going to describe what happened that night using a level of detail that will put you off ever giving this book to your parents to read, but at the same time I won't ramp it up to a level in which you'll feel like you're reading an excerpt from a black market porn magazine. In short, I'll give you a bit of sleaze, but I won't go overboard.

Let's cut to the hotel room. I was in this room with these two beautiful women, and I could hardly believe my luck. The room wasn't that big; the bed took up most of the space, but it was suitable for the occasion. Fresh sheets, folded towels, a glass bowl with sweets in the corner, etc. There were also large mirrors on the walls surrounding the bed, which I loved. Come to think of it, it was probably some kind of sex hotel, but that didn't really sink in at the time. I was too buzzing on nerves and alcohol to fully comprehend the entirety of the situation. I hope you can forgive me for that.

After taking a shower, I lay on the bed with my hands behind my head in a fake relaxed pose, waiting for the two of them to take their shower and get ready. They both got undressed at the end of the bed, and this energy began to run through me. The sheer sensation of being in a room with not one, but two, naked women was doing things to me that I could never describe. There was giggling and whispering behind the bathroom door as they washed together, and then after about ten minutes or so they reappeared, their naked bodies glistening.

Flesh.

So much smooth, buttery flesh, dear reader. That's what I remember the most. Firm flesh, wobbly flesh, bouncing flesh...it was all there, right on top of me, coming from both sides.

Hair.

Hair seemed to be everywhere. Not body hair, I must say, but the silky dark locks of hair that flowed from their heads as they hovered above me. It tickled my face, it fell to the bedsheets, it clung to the sweat on my abdomen.

Nails.

At various times, I actually felt as though I was being attacked by a couple of cats. Long, sharp, painted, lacquered, manicured nails tickled and scratched my trembling limbs and orifices, embellishing my skin with a network of scarlet lines.

Mirrors.

The mirrors heightened the experience for me in ways you cannot even begin to imagine. I could see my reflection all around me as I bounced around and turned around, grabbing and thrusting into these gorgeous curves. My pumping was presented to me everywhere I looked, reflected from these long, polished mirrors, allowing me to see myself from angles I'd never seen myself from before. Oh, it was bliss. Absolute bliss. Nothing was off limits; I had the time of my life.

Is that enough detail for you? No? Well, I'm sorry. If you want more filth, you'll have to go and get a copy of Fifty Shades of Grey, or something. And if that was too much detail for you, well...go and grab yourself a copy of Wind in the Willows.

This was the memory that popped into my head, dear reader, as I sat in my apartment with these Neurodes in front of me. *This'll do the trick*, I thought. *This'll get the papers talking about me, this'll get my name back up in flashing lights.*

Part of me didn't even believe that they were going to work. As I sat there, playing with these wires and pads, I just couldn't quite fathom how my memory of this event could travel through them onto the app. I was cynical, let's say.

Nevertheless, I followed the instructions to the letter. After sticking the pads to my head—no shaving necessary, which is also impressive—I plugged the Neurodes into the headphone socket of my smartphone, opened up the app, pressed the "upload" button, closed my eyes, and then summoned up the memory of that night in the hotel with as much detail as I could recall.

The instructions make it very clear that you have to visualize your memory as detailed and accurately as possible, in order for the app to be able to produce a clear, watchable video clip from it. This is where those mirrors helped me out.

Remember I told you that there were mirrors on the walls surrounding the bed in the hotel? Well, those mirrors helped me to recall some very clear images of that night, enabling me to produce a very lucid slideshow of events. Furthermore, the mirrors allowed me to be in the NeuroStar video. Let me explain. If it weren't for those mirrors, my memory of the threesome would've been a gonzo-type thing. I mean, everything would've been seen through my eyes, resulting in memories and images featuring only the two women. Do you get what I mean? Do you get what I'm saying here? Thanks to the mirrors, I was included in what I saw that night; I was part of the video.

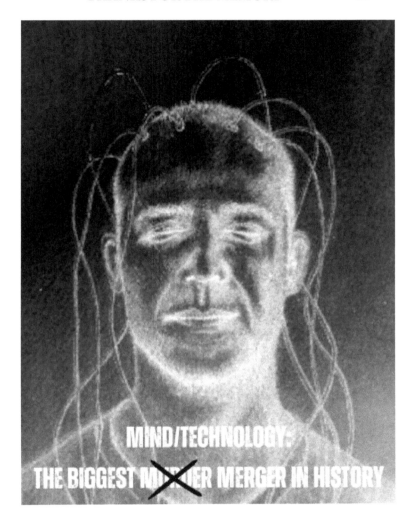

Once done, once I'd strained my brain and exhausted every recollection I had of that lusty night, I opened my eyes and peeled off the annoying little Neurodes.

Then I looked at my phone.

Would you believe me, dear reader, if I told you that everything I was previously thinking about and visualizing was right there, on the screen in front of me? Well, you bloody should do, because it's true! There it was! Right there! A video clip of me and the girls on the NeuroStar app, ready to upload onto the public timeline.

I pressed upload.

Laughter came out of me immediately afterwards, huge belly laughs as I stared down at the screen, watching my night of sexual antics being displayed for every keyboard warrior to check out.

I think I may have spent another five minutes or so on the app, scrolling down through other people's memory vids until I got bored. After that, I turned off my phone, brushed my teeth, and went to bed.

Little did I know, I'd just made the biggest mistake of my life.

* * *

Nothing much happened for a while. I got a few bookings at some new clubs in District 7, and immersed myself in my work. I revised my comedic routine, wrote some new jokes, and enjoyed the extra bit of money that these new gigs were bringing in.

It wasn't until I met up with Luke one afternoon, that everything fell into place. Luke is an old friend of mine who runs a bar called Velvet Lizard over in District 5. He's a tall man with a bald head, and he's got these wise eyes that stare out at you as if they know something you don't. To me, he resembles a taller, trimmer version of Uncle Fester from The Addams Family, and believe me, I point this out to him as much as possible. Old Luke is a bit crafty, and you could call him nosy, too. My other nickname for him is Yellow Pages, because he always seems to know everything about everyone.

'Well, hello stranger,' he grinned, as he saw me walking through the door.

'How ya doin', Luke?'

After wiping a glass and putting it on a shelf behind him, he gestured for me to sit on a stool right at the end of the bar.

'Could be better, could be worse. What will it be?'

'I'll have a Heineken, I think.'

'Coming right up, squire.'

There were two or three other people sat at the bar, but they were oblivious to my presence. Heads down towards their screens, they were tapping, tapping, tapping, scrolling, scrolling, scrolling away as though they couldn't get enough memes and images in front of their eyes. A couple of twenty-somethings were playing pool in the corner, minding their own business, and some electronic pop music was coming out of the overhead speakers.

'It's been a while,' said Luke, placing the drink in front of me.

'It certainly has. How's business?'

'Steady. Got my regulars in here, along with a couple of new bands.'

'Nice,' I said, glancing over at the small stage behind me. 'Any stand-up shows lately?'

Luke nodded. 'Occasionally.'

I could see it in his eyes that he had something he wanted to bring up, something he wanted to discuss but was slightly hesitant to do so. His powerful jaw was flexing as it often did in these moments, and a micro-grin was visible on his lips.

'I've been quite busy just lately. Done a few gigs over in District 7.'

The grin broadened. 'So I've heard.'

'Oh, yeah?'

'Yeah, Bob told me that he'd booked you a couple of times.'

'Bloody hell, Luke. You know everybody.'

'I certainly do,' he said, looking down at the floor.

'Mr Yellow Pages.'

'Whatever you say.'

'What's so funny, then? Why the grin?'

'Huh, I don't know, it's...it's just such a funny way to get work.'

'What is?'

Looking up at me again, his head shiny under the bar lights, he said, 'The video.'

An odd feeling washed over me.

'Video?'

'Don't play dumb with me. You know what I'm talking about.'

Now, you might find this hard to believe, dear reader, but the video I uploaded to NeuroStar simply wasn't on my mind at this time. The Neurodes had been tucked away in a drawer for some time, and I hadn't checked the app at all. Hearing Luke mention the video like this had quite an effect on me.

'Oh, you've seen it,' I mumbled.

'Who hasn't?' shrugged Luke. 'Very entertaining. Good bit of marketing, too, I must say.'

Things were clicking into place. It suddenly dawned on me that all of my recent bookings over in District 7 had been due to the hype my video had created. The organisers and promoters must've watched it, then seen an opportunity. Not that anyone mentioned any of this to me.

'So it worked,' I mumbled, more to myself than to Luke.

'If that was your game plan, my friend, then yes. Those bookings in District 7 happened because of this new video of yours.'

Shameless pride filled my veins. 'You know me, Luke. Always a businessman.'

'Where did you meet those two honeys?' Luke then enquired, leaning closer towards me across the bar.

I gave my old pal the rundown of the story, juicy bits and all, trying my very best to make him as jealous as possible. Then, after answering a dozen questions he had about the fiasco, he told me that my services were required on Saturday.

'It'd be a pleasure, Luke. It's been a while since I performed here.'

'Well, I think I ought to book you while I have the chance. It looks as though you're in high demand again.'

Luke said this in a playful way, but I could see that there was at least a small part of him that believed it.

'You better believe it,' I grinned. Then downed my drink and left.

Things were looking up, so it seemed.

* * *

After that encounter with Luke, I began to check the NeuroStar app everyday. I didn't upload anything else, I just wanted to see what was happening with the sex video. The day I got back home from Luke's bar, the video had accumulated over six million views. Six million! I couldn't believe my eyes! There was me, on the screen, bouncing around with these two lovely women, and just underneath there were these huge numerical figures. Six million views, a similar amount of likes, and untold comments.

My initial assumption about this was that the video was taking off due to my preexisting celebrity status. And, after reading some of the comments, this assumption was confirmed. A lot of the people who'd left a comment were old fans, people who already knew who I was. They were mainly in good humour, with a bit of shock and surprise here and there. Most people saw the video as a kind of joke or prank, although there were a few comments from prudish types who disapproved of the explicit content. I knew nothing about the NeuroStar rules and guidelines at this point, but it was pretty clear to me that they had no problem with videos of this nature being on their platform.

I would later find out why.

Another couple of weeks passed, and the clip showed no sign of slowing down. None at all. The views reached ten million, the likes and shares almost the same, and it was at this point that I realised it had gone viral. A couple of people stopped me on the street. Can you believe that? It was like the good old days, all over again. I was walking down 142 Street one evening, on my way to the convenience store to get a phone top-up voucher and some chocolate, and I heard this voice from over the road.

'Ten out of ten, pal! Good job! When's the sequel?'

I turned to see this muggy-looking bloke smiling at me from the other side of the street, with a dumb admiration painted all over his face. I knew at once what he was referring to, so I said, 'You rent the room, I'll get the women.' I'm well accustomed to a bit of heckling, you see. It's part of my job. The bloke laughed, then wandered off.

A few days later, I travelled over to Central Boulevard to shop for a couple of items. Central Boulevard is a big wide street with loads of hotels and shops and that, and there's this paved section in the middle where people sit on benches. You get skateboarders there trying to do their tricks, and you see the occasional street performer at weekends. Anyway, I was walking down the main drag, and a group of teenagers recognized me.

'Whaahheeyy! Bouncing Blagden! It's you!'

This was the precise moment that I discovered I had a new nickname: Bouncing Blagden. Yes, in case you're wondering, it was annoying. Hearing that stupid name being shouted at me on the street by a group of gawky teenagers...yes, of course, it was a highly irritating experience. But the thing is, I'm a comedian. I'm a comedian who pokes fun at people for a living, a comedian who has even created a few nicknames for other people during the course of my career, so, as the Americans like to say, I ate humble pie and took it on the chin.

The work kept flowing in, too. There was no doubt now that the extra bookings were due to my internet fame, because organisers were openly stating so. Walking through the doors of Club Flamingo one Friday night, Rog, the owner, stood up from one of the tables and greeted me.

'Reed! Good to see ya.'

'Hello, Rog. How are you?'

'All the better for seeing you. It's gonna be a full house tonight, pal. Every table's sold and reserved.'

Rog is an old-school type. He's got this pathetic comb-over hairstyle, just a few strands of greying hair gelled over his scalp, and these thick glasses. His gravelly smoker's cough gives him a deep tone, and his confident demeanour gives off the impression that he's seen it all. I'd never heard him talk like this before, though.

'Reserved tables?'

'Just for you, Reed. People are booking tables just for you.'

Looking around Club Flamingo, I could see these little plastic signs all over the place. Little white signs that'd been put on the tables surrounding the elevated stage.

'Fucking hell, Rog. Since when have people been reserving tables here?'

Smiling over the top of his spectacles, Rog replied, 'Ever since I started booking star performers. You're on the rise again, Reed. You need to acknowledge that.'

After a short pause, I replied, 'Does that mean I should be getting paid more?'

Rog's bespectacled eyes shot off to the side at this, in avoidance. 'Err, well, let's not get too carried away. I mean...'

'Too carried away? I'm seeing reserved tables, and posters of me all over the walls with the words "Internet Sensation" printed on them!'

This was true, dear reader. I was seeing these posters of me around the club that Rog had plastered up, and the main photo was of me holding a microphone, performing somewhere during my old glory days. And just underneath me, the words "Internet Sensation" had been superimposed. This was something else, it really was.

'Alright, look,' croaked Rog, 'put on a good show tonight, and then we'll have a chat and discuss your salary.'

'Deal,' I said, suppressing a satisfied smile.

Sticking to my promise, I put on a good show that night. Some of my new jokes got the audience roaring and yelling: Who's the most popular man at a nudist colony? The man who can carry a coffee in both hands, as well as five donuts. And, for the sake of a few old timers I spotted down at the tables, I told an old favourite of mine: How do you get your girlfriend to scream during sex? Phone her, and tell her about it.

Reg was happy with how it went down, and he stuck to his end of the promise: a sizeable pay rise! I was lapping it up, I won't lie. Lapping up the money, lapping up the attention, and lapping up the sheer excitement of it all. It was like being born again. A born-again comedian!

The cynical part of me was speculating about the possible negatives, though. Mainly concerning the two women in the video, I mean. Had they seen it? Were they embarrassed? Were they enjoying the attention like me? Were they trying to find me? I hadn't performed at Bar 5 for a while at this point, not since I uploaded the video, and I was kind of avoiding the place for fear of bumping into them. I didn't know whether they were regulars there, but they definitely weren't strangers to the place.

On the other hand, part of me was tempted to try and find them. Would they be up for another meet? Another video, even? This was crazy talk, though, wasn't it? The wild ideas of a dirty, opportunistic, low-life comedian. But still, I hadn't ruled out the possibility of a second encounter with them. The problem was, though, I didn't get either of their phone numbers that night. Stupid bastard, I know. You don't need to tell me. The only thing I had to go on was a vague recollection of one of them mentioning their address, but I couldn't quite remember it. Was it Lombard Street, or Lombard Walk? Number 43, or 63? Or was that completely wrong? I just couldn't remember it, mainly due to the alcohol I'd consumed that night.

In short, I didn't have a clue whether the two girls had seen the video or not, and I didn't have a clue how they'd react to it if they did. Leaving them alone seemed like the best option, and so that's exactly what I did.

I now had bigger fish to fry, after all. I was going up in the world.

* * *

Excerpt from a newspaper article, printed in The Mapharno Times

The high-profile lawsuit involving Mr Bill Goldschmidt, CEO of the NeuroStar Corporation, and one of his junior employees, Mr Sam Beckett, is due to enter its second hearing at Mapharno City High Court today.

Sam Beckett initiated the lawsuit after his boss, Mr Goldschmidt, allegedly assaulted him in the office of the main company building. Goldshmidt's defence lawyers claim that Mr Beckett is guilty of negligence, due to the fact that the junior employee accidentally wiped the company hard drive, deleting hundreds of valuable files. Mr Beckett's lawyer has so far avoided comment on this detail of the case, and has instead focused on the horrific physical attack carried out by the CEO.

Bill Goldschmidt's reputation has been tarnished for some time, after allegations of violent misconduct surfaced at one of his former companies several years ago. This previous incident, involving a similar burst of lost temper in the workplace, never made it to court, but has nevertheless stuck in the minds of many, giving the millionaire entrepreneur a tainted image he is struggling to shake off.

Mr Goldschmidt has so far neither confirmed nor denied that he physically assaulted Mr Beckett, but today's hearing may include an official statement from one of his many hired lawyers. During yesterday's hearing, Mr Goldschmidt's defence team highlighted the detrimental impact the employee's blunder has had on the company, due to the irretrievability of the missing files. The software behind the NeuroStar app is surprisingly rudimentary, stated the Goldschmidt defence team, meaning that many, if not all, of the deleted files cannot be replaced. The company's software technician attended yesterday's hearing, and also made a statement...

End of Excerpt

Ironically enough, the problems began when another woman entered the scene. The attention that I was getting didn't just come from nightclub promoters, punters, and idiots on the street, you see. Women were suddenly finding me rather attractive, too. It was the elevated profile, of course. I know that. I was under no illusion. I consider myself to be semi-good looking, but I knew that these women simply enjoyed being part of the sensational buzz that surrounded me.

However, despite my knowledge of this, I certainly wasn't in the habit of turning them away. Yeah, I had some fun, in case you're wondering. I had a few one-night stands, but so what? Does that make me bad? Well, if it does, so be it. This all changed one night, anyway, when I met a darling of a young lady in one of the upmarket venues in District 7.

This place was more of a restaurant, really, not a nightclub. It was full of posh-looking customers sitting at tables piled up with food and bottles of wine, most of them wearing button-up shirts and shiny shoes, and all that kind of thing. It made me a bit nervous, actually, performing in there. There were definitely no crass posters of me hanging up in this place, it was all tablecloths and chandeliers and framed abstract paintings and the like.

Did they actually know who I was? The manager of the place phoned me up one Thursday afternoon, offering me a one-hour slot at the weekend. I didn't ask too many questions, and neither did he. Whether he'd seen my NeuroStar video or not, I had no idea. When I walked through the door, I knew right away that I was going to have to omit some of my edgier jokes. The routine I was doing at the time included jokes like: What do you call a leper in the bath? Porridge! I mean, come on! How could I have come out with a gag like that in front of a group of wine-sipping, tie-wearing, upmarket toffs?

It was a nerve-racking gig, to say the least, but I got through it in one piece. I got a few laughs, as well. To my surprise, they enjoyed my joke about an insecure husband: 'Tell me something that will make me happy and sad at the same time,' said a man, to his wife. 'Your penis is bigger than your brother's,' she replied. They're not all bad, you know, these posh types. It's just this overly-sophisticated impression that they sometimes give off, that's all. It can put you on the defensive back foot. Anyway, I even hung around for a while after my show was over, and ordered a glass of cabernet sauvignon from the bar. Pretty tasty, I must say, although not as tasty as the aforementioned darling of a young lady who came over and approached me.

Picture the scene: the stool I was sitting on had red velvet upholstery, the bartender was wearing a silk waistcoat, there were chandeliers up on the ceiling which I presume were crystal, glass bowls full of olives and cheese were artistically positioned along the polished surface of the bar, and then, to top it all off, a classy-looking young lady came over and stood next to me! What was going on? Was the world about to end?

'Hello, I'm Emily,' she said, with a toothy smile that wouldn't have looked out of place on a toothpaste commercial.

'Nice to meet you. I'm Reed.'

Again, I felt silly saying this, because she obviously had just watched my performance, and hence knew my name, but whatever.

'Mind if I join you?'

'Not at all. Take a seat.'

'I just wanted to tell you that I really enjoyed your show.'

Her dark eyes were melting me, and a sweet scent of expensive perfume emanated from her pale neck, making me dizzy with lust.

'Thank you very much. I don't usually perform in places like this, but I quite enjoyed it.'

She then said, 'You were wonderful.'

The way she said it, dear reader, you wouldn't believe. She was one of these women who oozed sexual attraction from every single pore, from every single movement of her well-proportioned body, and from every single fibre of her glorious being. Was I dreaming? Was this really happening? An upmarket stunner was coming on to me, giving me the movie star treatment! Oh, how my life had changed.

After buying her a drink, we chatted at the bar for a good hour or so. The usual small talk, I suppose, but every second of it was charged with an incredible spark of energy that flowed between us, every meaningless nicety dripping with a mutual, but unspoken, erotic connection. I didn't dare ask her to come to my apartment, or anything like that; a woman of this caliber would never agree to such a thing on a first meeting. But of course, I got her phone number. I simply had to. Let's put it this way: if I'd left that place without doing so, I would have deserved to have been hung, drawn, and quartered.

We went out on a couple of dates shortly after that. I took her to a pricey coffee shop in Central District on the first day, then we went to a semi-posh buffet place in District 3 for the second date. We seemed to click quite well, despite our class differences, and I could sense a relationship developing. But here's the thing: I slowly gathered, during the time we spent together, that she had no idea whatsoever about my online fame. She was oblivious to the viral video that I was a part of, and clueless to the fact that ten million people worldwide had seen me getting it on with two women at once (in actual fact, the figure was more like eleven million at this point).

More dates followed, and over the weeks and months, we grew closer and closer. My feelings for this girl intensified, her sex appeal losing none of its intensity, no matter how often I saw her. However, during this blissful romantic development between us, an unsettling panic was brewing inside me. *How would she react if she saw the threesome video? Would she get angry? Would she leave me and walk away?* These were the thoughts that haunted me as I lay in my bed at night, these were the questions that deprived me of sleep while Emily and I formed a loving bond.

Tell me: what would you have done, dear reader and valued friend, if you were in my shoes? It's obvious, isn't it? There was only one thing for me to do—delete the video!

So, that's exactly what I did. Pulling the sweaty bedsheets off of me one night, after tossing and turning without sleep for at least two hours, stressing about the ridiculous situation, I grabbed my phone and opened up the NeuroStar app. With a few taps and scrolls, there it was, the infamous viral sex video right there on the screen of my smartphone, with all the astronomical viewing figures and share figures displayed underneath it. After humming and hawing for a while, wondering what kind of impact the deletion of such a thing might have on my comedic career, I plucked up some blind courage and pressed the delete button.

It felt surprisingly good; soothing, even. It was like getting rid of some incriminating evidence, throwing a huge weight off my shoulders. I even uninstalled the NeuroStar app, for good measure.

After the deed was done, I returned to bed, pulled the sheets back over me, and slept the way a man does when he has a clear conscience and a clear head.

'No more NeuroStar,' I muttered to myself, in the dark—or so I thought.

* * *

If I remember rightly, and I think I do, a few days later I performed at a club called Seventeen Saloon. It's like a rock tribute band place. You see these middle-aged rocker types in there with ponytails and leather jackets, and all that. I pulled out my filthy material, and put on a decent show. I had everyone in stitches with this joke about a nun who...oh, you probably don't want to hear it. Anyway, the club was cheering and crying out for more, which was good enough for me.

After it was all over, I ordered a drink at the bar, as I often do, and watched this band perform a couple of Guns and Roses songs. They were terrible, if I'm honest. The band members were too young and geeky to pull it off properly, and it just didn't come together right. After the second song, I pulled out my phone and began to check my emails out of boredom.

Most of my emails were the usual spammy shite, of course. "You've been selected for this!" "You've won this new voucher!" "You're eligible for a loan!" "I am an African prince, and I have $3 million that I need to transfer to a bank account."

I mean, seriously, who falls for this nonsense? Anyway, I was scrolling down through this sea of spam and garbage, deleting them one by one, when I came across a sender's email address that looked something like this: admin@neurostar.com

Alarm bells started ringing, dear reader, as soon as I saw it. It was like a premonition, or an intuition, whatever they call it. I had this uncomfortable feeling rising up in my gut, like a nervous tickle that I didn't like one bit.

I opened the email.

Transcribing the entire email here, word for word, would bore you too much. Instead, I'll simply tell you the gist of what it said. In basic terms, the NeuroStar Corporation (and by this point, I was very aware that it was a corporation because it said so in almost every sentence in the email) had made it very clear, using extremely formal and overly intimidating language, that I had an obligation to re-upload my memory onto their platform post haste (within 14 days, to be precise). It was explained to me in this stern email, using this complicated legal jargon that big companies like to use, that there's this clause in the terms and conditions of the NeuroStar contract (the contract that everybody agrees to by ticking a little box, without reading a single word of it, just like I did) which states that if the company wishes to retain a certain video clip and keep it on the website, it shall remain on the website whether the creator of the clip likes it or not.

I'm paraphrasing here, of course. It wasn't worded like that, it was written with these overly-technical phrases and sentences like: "The company retains the right under certain circumstances to...blah, blah, blah." And: "As stated in section 14 of the user agreement, by uploading content to the

NeuroStar Corporation platform, the user is giving the company permission to...blah, blah, blah." And: "If the clip in question is not re-uploaded to the NeuroStar platform within 14 days of this correspondence, the company is legally entitled to...blah, blah, blah." The email was full of sentences like that, you know? All that technical jargon, the stuff that gives you a headache after about two seconds. But what I'm trying to tell you here, dear valued reader and friend, is that I was royally shitting myself. It was rapidly dawning on me that if I didn't re-upload my memory onto the NeuroStar app within the given timeframe, I'd be in some pretty serious trouble.

Now, if you're anything like me, you'll be wondering why NeuroStar bothered kicking up such a fuss about this video. The reason is very simple: money. Money makes the world go round, as they say, and the internet world is no different. My video was making the company some serious dough through ad revenue and stuff like that, and popular videos also help draw people towards the website and spend more time on it, resulting in more subscriptions and clicks and ads and whatever else. In other words, my viral video was a money-spinner, and they didn't want to let it go. I hit them where it hurt that night when I deleted the video, and business people don't like to be hit like that.

But look, here's the thing: it's my memory. My memory belongs in my head, not in some businessman's pocket. How can a corporation own someone's memory? That doesn't seem right at all, does it? And don't look at me like that. I know what you're about to say. You're about to say, 'Well, Reed, you *did* choose to share your memory with the rest of the world. Your memory can't be *that* precious and personal to you if you chose to share it like that. OK, smartass, I suppose you've got a point, but...still, how can it be right? Even if I chose to share it, surely I should have a right to take it down when I feel like doing so?

'Are you OK, pal? You look like you've seen a ghost.'

Looking up from the email, I saw this rocker-type bloke leaning towards me with a drink in his hand. He had a concerned look on his face, like he was worried about me in some way.

'Err, yeah, I'm OK mate. Thanks,' I replied.

'The beer isn't that bad, is it?' he joked.

It must've been weird for the man to see me sitting there with this mortified expression, because I'd been up on stage telling jokes twenty minutes earlier.

'No, no, it's not that. I just, err...I just need to get some air.'

Jumping off my stool, I literally ran out of Seventeen Saloon, overcome with this horrible nausea.

Uploading that video didn't seem like a very good idea anymore.

* * *

How did I respond to this threatening email? I hear you ask. What action did I take? Well, I did what any other law-abiding, responsible citizen would do in such circumstances: I deleted the email, and pretended that I'd never seen it. Don't tut at me like that! You would've done the same thing, wouldn't you? Be honest. My planned alibi, in case I needed one, was that the email had landed in my spam folder. Simple.

Meanwhile, Emily and I continued to meet every week, going to restaurants and coffee shops and stuff, and our relationship blossomed. I began to miss her presence when she wasn't there, sending her messages every single day, and thinking about her all the time. OK, look, I won't beat about the bush, I'll just come out and say it, shall I? I was falling in love with her. There it is. Are you satisfied now? Funny, sleazy Reed Blagden was falling in love! It's crazy, I know, but I was. She was the first truly attractive woman I'd ever dated, and it was having a strong effect on me. She had class, *real* class, and this delicate presence that did something to the core of my being. I'm not entirely sure what she saw in me, maybe the whole celebrity thing swept her up a bit, you know? Whatever. I wasn't complaining.

With a certain degree of mental effort, I managed to convince myself that the NeuroStar business was nothing to worry about. My entire focus was on Emily, and when I wasn't with her, I concentrated on writing some new jokes and observational material to include in my new act. Delusion will only get you so far, though, and after about two and a half weeks, another email landed in my inbox.

No prizes for guessing who it was from, I'm afraid. And this time, the threatening legal jargon from my good friends over at the NeuroStar Corporation had ramped up a notch. This time, I was seeing words like: "breach", "misdemeanor", "contractual obligation", and "prosecution". There were also sentences like: "The company retains the right to take action against you...", "Your lack of correspondence grants us authority to...", and 'We have forwarded this case to the Mapharno City Police Department".

It was this last sentence, dear reader, that had me shaking in my boots. The Mapharno City Police Department? Really?

We're talking about social media here, for crying out loud! The police? But you know what? Despite all the fancy words and scary talk, and despite the fact that I was a bit scared at this point, I still didn't quite believe that a corporation like that would actually take action against me. It was all a bit far-fetched for me, a bit too fantastical for me to truly accept.

Besides, there was nothing I could really do at this point. The 14-day window had passed, and they were claiming that the case had been forwarded on to the police. Were they bluffing? Was it simply a case of corporate bullying? A big corporation trying to bully a powerless citizen into doing something they weren't legally obligated to do?

That's what I kept telling myself.

* * *

Guess what? They weren't bluffing. The emails from NeuroStar fizzled out, which came as a great relief, but they were soon replaced by emails and letters from my local district constabulary. The bastards actually went ahead and reported me to the police. Can you believe that? They actually did. The letters arriving at my door had these official stamps on the envelopes and everything, and the letters themselves were printed on this creamy, quality paper that gave off the impression that they weren't messing around.

I should, at this point in the story, tell you a little bit more about my apartment. I basically live in a small room within a large shared building. There are ten rooms within the building, which consists of three floors, and my landlady, Meredith, lives down on the ground floor with her cats. I live on the second floor. The building is situated down a narrow alleyway in District 1, and is accessed by a set of metal shutters. Sounds shady, doesn't it? I suppose it is, really, but I've never had any dramas. The shutters open up to a communal downstairs lobby, where all residents can leave their shoes and bicycles and stuff.

Meredith's a decent woman, and she's looked after me well enough during the few years that I've lived there. She's in her sixties, has been a widow for several years, and she spends most of her time watching daytime TV and treating her cats as though they were human babies, or something.

I'd never had a problem with her before, and neither had she with me, but when the postman started delivering these letters with the MCPD stamp on them, her attitude towards me altered somewhat.

'This arrived for you today,' she said one afternoon, as I opened the shutters and walked into the downstairs lobby.

She was holding the first letter that the police had sent me, the big stamp clearly displayed on the top, and there was this distrustful glint in her eyes that I'd never seen before.

'Thank you, Meredith,' I said, taking the letter from her.

She didn't say anything the first time, but after the second and third letters arrived, her silent concern became vocal. She caught me downstairs one morning, as I was going out to get some bread.

'Is everything OK, Reed?'

'Yes,' I said, with a nervous chuckle.

'I couldn't help but notice you're getting a lot of letters from the MCPD.'

'Oh, that. Yeah, don't worry about that. It's fine. I, err...I lost my bag the other week, and I reported it missing.'

Meredith took a sharp intake of breath, displaying a kind of motherly concern that she has now and then for her residents, her voice softening. 'Your bag? Oh, dear. Was there anything valuable in it?'

'Err, well, my laptop was in there.'

'Your laptop? Oh, no! Do you think you'll get it back?'

Thinking on my feet, I then spent the next five minutes or so fabricating this lame story about me working with the police to try and locate the whereabouts of my laptop. It was pathetic, but I think she believed it.

In reality, though, the letters were formal requests for me to report to my local police station in order to discuss the charge that'd been put against me. My response: avoidance.

Ignorance is bliss, as they say. Letters get lost in the post, don't they? How could they be so sure that I was receiving their letters? Anything can happen to a letter. They can fall out of a postman's bag, they can get chewed up by dogs, they can get lost in sorting offices, etc, etc. Irresponsible? Maybe. Stupid? Perhaps. But look: those assholes over at the NeuroStar Corporation were taking the piss, and I wasn't going to bow down to them that easily.

How many letters were there in total? Let me think...about four or five, if I remember rightly. They got progressively sterner and more authoritative each time, of course, but every time I opened one of them I thought, *Fuck those wankers. It's* my *memory!*

Things finally came to a head late one evening, after I returned home from a gig in District 10. I was taking my shoes off downstairs, when I heard a voice behind me.

'There was a police officer here this afternoon, Reed.'

I turned to see my landlady, Meredith, standing behind me, looking cold and cross.

'Really? Have they found my laptop?'

'No, I don't think they have, Reed.' She looked insulted at this point. 'In fact, he didn't seem to know anything about a laptop when I asked him.'

'Huh, that's typical. You know how they operate sometimes. The officer they sent here probably wasn't informed about the full details.'

'He didn't look very pleased, Reed. And he told me to tell you that you need to report to the station ASAP.'

'Oh, right,' I said, trying to look bright and happy. 'This sounds promising.'

I could tell that she really, *really* wanted to press me for some details, to ask me what this was really all about, but my innocent act was played well enough to hold her back.

'I'll get on the phone to them as soon as I get upstairs,' I lied. 'Find out what's going on.'

'Yes, I think you should,' she said, before returning to her whining cats.

This was the turning point for me. Things were escalating to a whole new level, and I knew that I had to take some kind of action. Keeping a slow, casual pace, I climbed the stairs to my room, but as soon as the door was closed, I found a bag and began frantically stuffing clothes and toiletries into it. Once that was done, I quietly went back downstairs and walked out into the alley without making a sound.

Thankfully, it was a warm, dry night, so I could comfortably work out what I was going to do as I traipsed along the alley towards the main road. My first instinct was to phone someone I knew, and ask to sleep on their sofa for the night. It was the obvious thing to do, but as I mentally went through my list of friends, the idea fell apart. Most of my friends are club owners, of course, and...well, I won't lie to you, dear reader, nightclub owners are quite renowned for dabbling in dodgy business. Even better, you may be thinking, but the thing is, I didn't want to lead the police to my friends' doorsteps. I was technically a fugitive at this point, and none of my friends needed that kind of hassle.

Luke, for example, often keeps counterfeit money in the cellar of his place in District 5. Rog used to sell ecstasy pills from the office of Club Flamingo, and everybody else I could think of broke the law in some way or another. Calling Emily and asking her was out of the question, because she'd naturally wonder why I couldn't sleep at my apartment. I mean, shit, this whole mess occurred due to the fact that I was hiding something from her, so it would've been ridiculous of me to head over to her place.

Extreme situations call for extreme measures, I think that's how the saying goes. In the end, I decided that I was going to have to rough it for the night. There's this big abandoned block of flats on the other side of District 1, about a twenty-minute walk from my apartment, and I decided to head over there. Bit of a drastic move, some might say, but I needed somewhere quiet and secluded so that I could work out what I was going to do.

If I could make it over there without being spotted, I would have a decent amount of time to think.

This derelict block is right on the corner of a main road, which was not ideal, but I managed to haul my ass over the security fence during a brief lull in passing traffic, and I don't think anyone saw me.

I've got this weird fascination for derelict buildings. Perhaps that's the real reason I ended up over there that night. There's something mysterious about them, isn't there? Seeing these crumbling structures and knowing that people used to live there, sleep there, eat there, and go back there after work everyday, it...it fills me with this strange awe. Climbing up the stairwell of this place, I looked around at the flaking paintwork and decrepit lightbulbs dangling on tattered cords, trying to imagine what it all looked like back in the day.

Splintered doorways led through to old dusty apartments that used to be people's homes, fallen TV sets covered in rat shit, frayed sofas with spider's webs between the cushions, stray cats nibbling on bones from takeaway boxes, that kind of thing. Call me weird if you like, but I love all that. I mean, one day there's a building that people call home, they cook there, bathe there, drink there, fuck there, get dressed for work in the morning there, and then...it all turns to dust, a dusty shell with cockroaches and cats and insects and fugitives wandering about the place.

Anyway, I digress.

Reaching the top floor of this block, I was drawn towards a hollowed-out apartment on the north side. The living room windows of this place were gone, along with a section of wall on either side of the frame, and I was greeted by this panoramic cityscape as I walked towards the edge of the room. Mapharno City was laid out before me in all its nighttime glory, and it damn near took my breath away.

Say what you want about cities and skyscrapers, about how they pollute and ruin the environment and what have you, but you can't deny that they look good at night. There's nothing quite like a gleaming, luminescent cityscape at night, I tell you. I was lost in it for quite some time, dear reader, meditating on the flashing lights of the vast metropolis, feasting my eyes on the yellows and whites and blues, momentarily forgetting about the awful mess that I'd gotten myself into.

My respite was broken by the sound of my phone ringing.

Anyone with two brain cells to rub together knows that you should switch off your smartphone if you're on the run from the police, so it appears that I may be cerebrally challenged. Pulling the bloody thing from my pocket, I expected to see an unknown number, a police station landline or something, but when I looked at the screen I realised it was actually worse than that—it was Emily.

This was worse because if it had been the fuzz, I could've simply not answered it. I could've let it ring and ring, and then switched it off afterwards. But I couldn't do that with Emily, no way. I had to pick up as I always did, and with that came the possibility of having to answer a few awkward questions.

A day in the life of Reed Blagden. You wouldn't want to be me, I tell you that now.

'Hello?' I said, as calmly as possible.

'Hello, baby. How are you?'

That voice. That smooth, silky voice. It made it all worthwhile.

'I'm fine, baby. How are you?'

'I'm OK. Do you want to go somewhere tonight? Have a drink somewhere?'

My thoughts were racing at this point, as you can imagine. What was I going to say? Should I be honest with her? No, that would be relationship suicide. Should I be semi-honest with her? Maybe. Perhaps I could explain the situation, but say that the video in question was something a bit more innocent, something non-sexual? Hhmm, a definite maybe. On the other hand, should I just outright lie, and say that I'm too tired to go out tonight? Pretend that none of this is happening?

Which option do you think I chose? Again, no prizes for guessing.

'Babe, I'd love to see you tonight, but I'm absolutely shattered. I had a tough crowd tonight, minimal laughs, and—'

'It's OK, I understand. Get some rest.'

'Yeah, that's what I need. I need a good night's sleep, that's all. I tell you what, let's go out tomorrow night and I'll treat you to something nice. How about that?'

'That sounds nice, honey. Recharge your batteries for me, and give me a call tomorrow.'

'Will do. Love you, babe.'

'Love you, too. Sleep well.'

Sure, I felt a bit bad, but sometimes it's easier to just tell a little white lie, isn't it? I switched the phone off after that, then sat down on the concrete floor near the crumbling window frame, looking out at the sky, pondering my situation. Weighing up my options, I considered what the consequences might've been if I handed myself into the police. What exactly did they plan on doing, anyway? Were they going to force me to re-upload my memory? Were they going to pull out a set of those stupid Neurodes, and aggressively stick them on my head? Was that even legal?

It probably was, I concluded. Technology was becoming king in Mapharno City, an unstoppable force. As I've already mentioned, people live their lives on social media in this city, and the online world is becoming more important than the offline world. They call it Dataism, I believe, and several scholars and commentators had already speculated that this new way of life would soon take over the land, including the legal system. I'm digressing, I'm getting way off track here, but what I'm saying is that in all probability, the MCPD would have the power to force me to re-upload my memory against my will.

Frightening, isn't it? The authorities having the power to get inside your head like that. Gazing out at the city lights and the purple night sky, I thought about this long and hard. Entering your brain, without your consent. Tapping into your grey matter, even though you've said no. This techno-absurdity was occupying my thoughts for a long while, this digital dilemma, and I began to consider the prospect of me staying on the run forever, living the life of a professional, nomadic fugitive.

Another part of me, however, was looking at the problem from a different angle. The authorities could tap into my brain and retrieve a memory, I reasoned, but they couldn't control what that memory was. The current technology didn't grant them the ability to enter my thoughts and look around;

instead, they could only force the Neurodes to my head, and command me to summon up the desired memory myself. This allowed for a certain amount of deception on my part.

Feeling as though I was on the brink of coming up with a solution to my problem, I continued to think along these lines. As I did so, I recalled an article that I'd read a long time ago concerning the accuracy of our memories. Hey, you're giving me that look again. Yes, I know, I'm a guttersnipe comedian; I'm a dirtbag with loose morals. But that doesn't mean that I don't read now and again, OK? Hear me out.

This article that I read, it was about the unreliability of the human brain, and how our memories are often rather inaccurate. It was pretty convincing. For example, have you ever re-watched a film that you haven't seen in years, and a certain scene comes up that you think you remember well? It could be a scene where two people are sitting at a table talking, or something like that. You might remember one of the characters wearing a tie, but when you re-watch the scene, you notice they're not wearing a tie. Or, you might remember one of them saying, "Marvellous job you did there", but when the scene comes on you hear them say, "Fantastic job you did there". I've heard this phenomenon being referred to as The Mandela Effect. Some people explain it by claiming that we live in The Matrix or something, but that's bullshit. It's due to the fact that our brains play tricks on us.

That's just one example, too. There's also the Pollyanna Principle. This is about how we tend to forget how bad certain experiences were in the past. We often recall our past experiences through rose-tinted spectacles, believing that our lives are better than they actually are. It's a psychological survival mechanism, I suppose. It's there to keep our spirits up. On top of that, there's also the scientifically-proven fact that eyewitness court statements are often unreliable. Certain experiments have been carried out in the past, where the test subjects have claimed they saw a red jumper even though it was blue, or they saw a person with short hair even though they had long hair, you know?

You can take that look off your face now. Just remember: despite my appearance and demeanour, there is a touch of sophistication in me.

So there I was, a fugitive sitting in this mouldy carcass of a building, trying to figure out how I was going to get myself out of this pickle, when this article popped into my head. After another moment's thought, I put two and two together and realised that the memory of my threesome that I'd uploaded onto NeuroStar probably wasn't very accurate at all. In all probability, it was a juiced-up, over-inflated, highly exaggerated version of what really happened that night. That's the honest truth.

This was bad news for my ego, because it meant that my wild night of passion probably wasn't as wild as I remembered it to be. It was good news in another sense, though, because if I could somehow retrieve an accurate memory of what happened that night, the resulting memory would be a less exciting, dulled-down version of the original one. The beauty of this was that a dulled down version of the memory would produce a less valuable video clip, a boring clip that would generate much less buzz and excitement than the first one. This, in turn, would reduce the likelihood of Emily stumbling upon it by accident. Furthermore, the authorities would have to let me go!

I could hand myself in, claim that I was willing to re-upload my memory, then, when push came to shove, I'd upload the drab, boring version. NeuroStar could then upload it to their platform if they so wished, but so what? It would probably flop.

These things are always easier said than done, though, aren't they? Even though I had a fairly decent plan, I had no idea how I was going to access my memory in a more accurate way. I tried the obvious first. I closed my eyes and thought about the memory in a more refined, acute manner, straining to remember any small details that may have escaped me the first time. It kind of worked, but not really. I mean, I remembered a couple of extra details about the night, like the fact that there was a red lampshade next to the bed, and that I told the girls one of my sleaziest, dirtiest jokes when we first got to the room in an attempt to loosen them up. I suppose you want to know what the joke is, don't you? OK, it was this: What's the difference between a Catholic priest and a zit? A zit will wait until you're sixteen before it comes on your face. Bad taste? Maybe. But hey, they found it funny.

None of this was enough, however; nowhere near enough. The main events were still the same in my mind, the same images and snapshots that were there before, most of them, in all likelihood, gross exaggerations of the truth. What I'm saying here, is that I couldn't improve upon the memory in any significant way on my own.

Sensing that I was getting nowhere fast, I let out a sigh of despair and slumped back on the floor. I was lying there on the dust and shit, feeling sorry for myself, staring up at the filthy ceiling. Falling into this sense of resignation and despair, I lay there like that for quite a while, looking up moronically at the mould patches above my head. Every now and then a lorry or a bus whizzed by outside on the main road, and there would be a bright flash whizzing across the ceiling as the headlights bounced around the room, then everything would fall into darkness again. It was quite soothing, in a way. Darkness, then light. Darkness, then light.

Now, this may sound a bit silly, but this intermittent light show on the ceiling reminded me of something. It reminded me of an eccentric, odd little club I used to perform in called The Crypt. It was over in District 4, and they always used to have dark-themed events in there. The management team was into gothic stuff, I think, or anything sinister and eerie. And they always made an effort when it came to lighting. When I performed there a couple of times, I felt as though I was in a theatre, not a club. Funny place, it was.

The acts were even funnier. I don't mean that in the humourous sense, either, I mean that they were weird. The act that I had to follow the first night I was there was a hypnotist act. What a freaky bastard! Mark Mesmer, his name was. Pretty good name for a hypnotist, actually, I must admit. And he did his job well, too. Dressed in a dark suit and tie, his hair immaculately combed and gelled, contact lenses in his eyes that gave them a reptilian appearance, he had people up on stage clutching onto the arms of chairs because they thought they were balancing on the edge of a cliff, or looking around in a state of panic because they thought a lion was lurking somewhere nearby. It was hilarious to watch.

We had a chat after my stand-up routine was over, and he was telling me more about his work. A lot of his income came from curing people of phobias. Can you believe that? People used to pay him for that kind of stuff. Good work if you can get it, I suppose.

Anyway, to cut a long story short, as I was thinking back to this odd club, I wondered whether I still had Mark Mesmer's number on my phone. Hypnotists are good at helping people retrieve lost memories, aren't they? That was my understanding.

Pulling myself up to a sitting position, I switched my phone back on and scrolled through my numbers, searching for Mark Mesmer's.

It was there.

You must remember, dear reader, that I hadn't spoken to this man for quite some time, so I was hesitant to call him late at night. How could I *not* call him, though, when I had such a huge problem on my hands? I checked the time: 22.07pm. Quite late for a weekday, but not ridiculously late. After a bit of indecision and mental debate, I took a deep breath and pressed call.

He answered after a few rings, and the conversation went something like this:

'Hello?'

'Hello Mark, it's Reed.'

A short pause, then, 'Reed?'

'Reed, the comedian. The stand-up comedian. I met you in The Crypt that time, remember?'

With slight confusion lacing his words, the hypnotist replied, 'Ah, Reed! Hello. How are you?'

This had to be played carefully and properly, dear reader. I couldn't tell the man that I was on the run from the police, could I? I didn't know him well enough. On the other hand, why would I be calling him during the night if everything was hunky-dory?

'I'm fine, Mark. Well, kind of fine. Sorry to call you out of the blue like this, but I need your help.'

'Oh yeah? What's the problem?'

'I don't quite know how to put this, but...do you have any experience in helping people retrieve lost memories?'

'Memory retrieval? Yeah, I've done that kind of thing before.'

Music to my ears, dear reader. Music to my ears.

'I need you to help me with a memory of mine. I want to remember a certain event in crystal clear clarity, as sharp as possible.'

Naturally, at this point, the hypnotist Mark Mesmer enquired about the nature of the memory in question. This is where the lies began, although my story was only a twisted, edited version of the truth.

I told Mark that I'd uploaded a saucy memory to NeuroStar, and that my girlfriend had then seen it and dumped me. I now wanted to contact one of the girls in the memory, but I needed to remember what her address was by recalling every detail of what happened that night. Initially, I considered the idea of completely omitting the NeuroStar element from the story, and simply telling him that I'd split with my girlfriend and wanted to find this other woman. This could've worked, but I knew that there was a strong possibility that Mark, being a worker on the nightclub circuit, had seen or heard about the NeuroStar video already, or would soon do so.

After digesting this madness, pausing again over the phone, Mr Mesmer said, 'When would you like to come over?'

What do you think I said to that, dear reader? A week next Tuesday?

* * *

That's right, I headed straight over there like a bullet out of a gun. That's quite an ironic way of putting it, too, because bullets could've come my way if the police had spotted me. I was still completely unwilling to comply at this point, a rebel of the techno-authoritarian system, and I wouldn't have stopped for any kind of officer.

As it turned out, though, the journey from the abandoned building to Mark Mesmer's apartment was smooth and uneventful. I paid cash for a taxi driver to take me over to District 2, where he lives, and I arrived on his doorstep after about twenty minutes. District 2 is pretty upmarket, a well-to-do area. It's a rich part of Mapharno City, even more so than District 7, and it has this quaint tranquility about it.

When I saw his pad, I was instantly jealous. After buzzing through a security gate, I walked up a set of marble stairs and knocked on his door. The sound of muffled footsteps grew closer, then the door opened up. Mark Mesmer stood there before me, wearing a loose cloth outfit, looking like some kind of charismatic, dark prince.

'Come in, Reed,' he smiled.

Swanky, I thought, as I walked around and took the place in. Expensive furniture was dotted around, framed figurative paintings were hung on the walls, candles were burning here and there, and an impressive-looking bookshelf took up an entire wall of the living room. I couldn't see any evidence of a woman living there, but at the same time, I could tell that the apartment had seen its fair share of female visitors.

'Good to see you again, Reed.'

Mark stood there in the living room, after having closed the front door, and I think it was the first time I'd ever seen him in clear light. The light in the apartment was quite dim, don't get me wrong, what with the candles and that, but for the first time, I could see his face without colourful strobes flashing across it. The reptilian contact lenses were absent, too, and I could see that he had piercing blue eyes, the colour of sun-illuminated waves.

'Likewise. Nice pad you have here, Mark. Very impressive.'

'Thanks very much. Do you want a drink?'

I said yes, and he told me to make myself at home while he prepared two cups of green tea. Once we were settled, he gave me a rundown of the procedure, and all that it entailed. After everything was explained, I got myself onto this white leather sofa in the corner of the room and waited while Mark made some preparations.

Sitting on a chair behind me, out of sight, he said, 'Like I said, what I'm going to do first is put you into a very light trance. An altered state of mind.'

With my eyes closed, I mumbled, 'OK.'

'Then I'm going to walk you through your memory, one step at a time.'

'OK, Mark. Go right ahead.'

Without any further messing around, Mark began whispering words into my ear, putting me into a more suitable frame of mind. I was hearing things like: 'As you sink down into your thoughts...', and 'Going deeper and deeper into yourself...', and 'Falling more and more inside your mind.' Mark Mesmer has this seamless voice, too, that makes you feel really calm and relaxed whenever you hear it. This, coupled with the vocab that he was using, had me falling into this cosy, trance-like state.

After a few minutes of this, Mark's voice seemed like it was drifting down to me from way up above somewhere. It felt like I was down in the depths of some deep cave, and he was up on ground level.

'Let's start at the beginning,' came the voice from above.

'I...I was at a bar.'

'Which bar were you at?'

'I was at Bar 5.'

'Whereabouts in the bar did you first see the girls?'

'I first saw them when I was up on stage, telling my jokes.'

'What time was it when you first saw them?'

'It must've been about...'

This is how it went, dear reader. Mark asked me question after question, guiding me through my memory of the night in a very precise, calculating manner. And because everything was being done properly and thoroughly, I was seeing things in a very different way. It was like being in an HD memory, everything in glorious technicolour, forgotten details and nuances bouncing up into my consciousness.

It became a bit embarrassing, I suppose, when we got to the hotel room part. He was asking me things like: 'What colour was their underwear?' 'Which one got undressed first?' 'Who was the first one to get on top?' 'Did you use lube?' 'What positions did you do?' 'Did either of them achieve orgasm?' 'Which one orgasmed first?' There were times, dear reader and valued friend, while I was hearing these questions drift down to me in my cave, when I thought he might've been having me on, joking around with me. But no, I honestly think that he was simply doing the job to the best of his ability, prising every last detail out of me as I'd requested. He was this all-knowing, trustworthy entity whispering from up high, and I was his obedient, honest, compliant subject down below.

Time was lost to me while I was in this dreamy state, so I can't tell you exactly how long this process went on for. After a while, the questioning stopped, however, and I began to hear words like *climb*, *rise*, and *resurface* being used in their place. Gradually, I had the sensation that I was being lifted higher and higher towards a different place in my mind, until I finally found the strength and control to open my eyes again.

'You did well there, Reed. Very well. And I've written everything down.' Tapping a gold fountain pen down on a pile of notes on his lap, he added, 'And we've got the address.'

The trance that I was in must've been pretty strong, because believe it or not, I was completely unaware that I'd given Mark Mesmer an address. The address wasn't really that important to me, though. The real reason I'd gone there to get hypnotized, I'm sure you'll remember, was to simply improve my overall memory of the whole night. I had to continue my lie to Mark, though, so I pretended to be over the moon about having this address at my disposal.

'Yes! We got it! Great work, Mark.'

'My pleasure,' he grinned.

He was just being nice here, really, because I'd agreed to pay him for his work. Pulling myself back up to a sitting position, I grabbed a wad of notes from my wallet and handed them over to him.

'Do you need a place to stay tonight, Reed?' he said, counting out the notes. 'It's getting pretty late.'

'Err, no, I'll be OK. Thanks, though.'

'Well, it was good to see you again. Let's not leave it so long next time, eh?'

'Definitely not. We'll go for a drink somewhere soon. I'll give you a call.'

That's how it went, dear reader. A few minutes later, I was back outside in the cool night air, considering what my next move might be. This isn't entirely true, actually. I knew exactly what my next move was, but I was too scared to jump right into it.

It's now or never, Reed. Stop being a pussy, and get on with it.

Phone in hand, I opened up a taxi app. Under destination, I typed the words: Central Police Station, Central District.

* * *

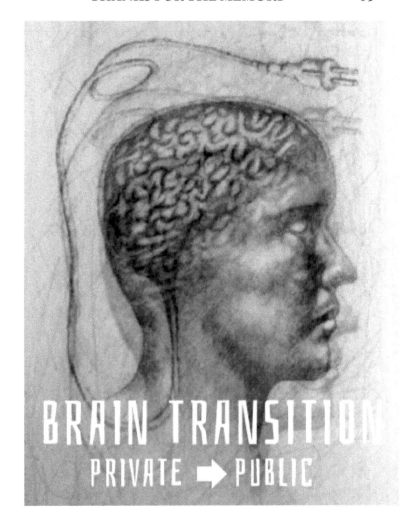

Central Police Station is a huge monstrosity of glass, concrete, and steel. Situated on a main road that cuts through the middle of Mapharno City, it has the appearance of a governmental headquarters, rather than a constabulary building. It has all these edges and sections to it, giving passersby the impression that some serious shit goes on within its walls. After the taxi dropped me off by the front steps, I felt like a vulnerable little lamb standing outside a juiced-up, mega abattoir. I was walking into the slaughter!

On the other hand, I was fairly confident that my plan was going to work. Standing outside on the steps, I accessed my memory of the night at the hotel and, now that Mark Mesmer had worked his magic on me, my recollection of the events was radically different. Whereas before I envisioned this wild, non-stop, energetic, porn star-style sex fest that went on for countless hours, with gymnastic bouncing and sweating and naked flesh undulating everywhere, I was now seeing things very differently. What I could see now in my mind's eye was more like a series of awkward grapples and shuffling, the kind of thing that occurs between two inexperienced teenagers the first time they find themselves together in the sack. To say it was toned down would've been an understatement. It was the kind of sex that drunken people have down alleyways after closing time, and that was being generous.

The kind of sex that wouldn't go viral, I thought, with satisfaction.

Lifting my head up high, and pulling my shoulders back, I walked through the main doors of Central Police Station, ready to face the music.

Don't get me wrong here, I don't like to promote stereotypes, but the officer sitting behind the desk at reception was a fat, lardy, doughnut-eating type. He was the kind of person that I would steam into if I saw him sitting in the audience of one of my gigs, the inevitable butt of a thousand fat jokes. There might have even been a box of iced-ring doughnuts under the counter, but I'm not totally sure. His bald dome of a head shone under the bright overhead lights, and his bagged eyes regarded me with a kind of tired, apathetic disdain.

'Can I help you?'

'I'm here to turn myself in.'

This made the fat bastard sit up straight.

'What crime have you committed?' he croaked.

Admittedly, this question stopped me in my tracks. What crime *had* I committed? What was the name for it? After a bit of fidgeting, I mumbled, 'Breach of contract.'

'Can I take your name, please?'

When my name popped up on the screen in front of him, there must've been a huge red flag next to it or something, because within minutes my possessions were taken away from me and put into sealed plastic bags, then I was thrown into a holding cell.

'Get your head down,' said this muscular guard, before closing the cell door. 'Someone will be here to see you in the morning.'

Get my head down, I did, dear reader. I was pretty exhausted by this point, after all, and the cell was comfier than the derelict building.

The sound of jangling keys woke me up the next morning, and I opened my eyes to see the guard from the previous night, accompanied by this slimy-looking man in a brown suit.

'Good morning. I'm Detective Rosenblum. I appreciate you turning yourself in like this, Mr Blagden. You've saved us a lot of time and money.'

'My pleasure,' I groaned, pulling myself upright on the foam bed.

Rosenblum looked down at me for a moment with a kind of detached compassion, the sort of demeanour you see on people playing a good cop routine. 'Your case is quite...unusual, Mr Blagden, so I want to make things as simple as possible.'

I nodded.

'I presume that you are willing to fully cooperate?'

I nodded again.

'Good. Well, normally, in the case of a breached contract, you would be facing a sizeable lawsuit. However, I've been in contact with the CEO of the NeuroStar Corporation this morning, Mr Bill Goldschmidt, and he has made it clear that if you are willing to re-upload this deleted memory, he will drop all charges against you.'

Fuckin get in there! I thought, although I continued to wear my serious poker face. 'I'm willing to re-upload the memory, sir. I'll do that.'

'Marvellous,' beamed Rosenblum. 'I'll let Mr Goldschmidt know, and we'll make arrangements post haste. In the meantime, I believe breakfast will be brought to you in around ten minutes or so.'

'Thank you, Detective.'

Rosenblum gave a brief nod, turned on his heel, then disappeared out into the corridor.

Not a bad start, I think you'll agree.

* * *

Hours passed, and I was still stuck in the cell. I thought they'd forgotten about me, but then someone came to deliver my lunch on a tray. I wolfed it down, even though it was tasteless. Then, shortly after that, an officer opened my cell door and escorted me down a series of corridors until we arrived in some kind of interview room. There was a desk in the corner, and some chairs lined up around the edge of the room. Rosenblum was sat on one of these chairs by the wall.

'Take a seat, Mr Blagden. The CEO of NeuroStar will be here shortly.'

'Thank you,' I muttered, plonking myself down next to the detective.

There were three of us in the room: me, Rosenblum, and the officer who'd escorted me from my cell. Detective Rosenblum was sorting through some paperwork on his lap, the other officer was standing by the door trying to look authoritative, and I was sitting there feeling rather anxious and jittery. Any minute now, this Bill Goldschmidt bloke would walk through the door, and I knew that he had a reputation for being fiery. Deep in my heart, I knew that he was going to be hard to handle. He was already angry at me for deleting the video, and who knew how he was going to react when he saw the replacement video?

Heavy footsteps echoed out in the corridor.

The officer by the door stiffened up, then pulled down the handle. A few seconds later, the biggest, burliest bastard I've ever seen in my life walked through the door. Bill Goldschmidt was a Neanderthal in a suit, a chunky, gruff, bull of a man. He had these wide shoulders underneath his suit, a protruding gut that looked as though it was full of raw meat, and a contemptuous look on his stubbly face that made the small hairs on my arms and neck stand endwise. Sometimes, you hear people talk about love at first sight. For me, seeing Goldschmidt for the first time, it was more like fear at first sight—or repulsion.

The man was flanked by two other people, one man, and one woman, both wearing suits and holding briefcases, and they entered the room as though they owned the land that the police station was built upon.

Detective Rosenblum played it cool and formal when confronted by this, but I could tell that he was also a little intimidated by the presence of these corporate high-flyers. 'You can use the table over there to set up the equipment,' he said, waving a hand towards the corner.

Bill Goldschmidt turned towards one of his assistants. 'Set up the laptop and the Neurodes,' he grumbled, in a tone that would've made Barry White sound like a eunuch on helium.

While everything was being set up, Rosenblum and Goldschmidt discussed certain legalities as though I wasn't even there. The animosity that Goldschmidt had for me was so intense, he couldn't bear to point his acerbic eyes towards me. He'd shot a brief, demonic glance in my direction when he first entered the room, but apart from that I was simply a stain in the corner that he tried his hardest to ignore. His hatred was so great, dear reader, that it had me wondering exactly how much money he'd lost due to my video clip being deleted. I mean, that clip must've been generating some serious cash for him to be this pissed off. Realising this, I felt a touch of regret for not monetizing the video myself somehow. I'm not that tech-savvy, but I know that you can put adverts on your videos and earn a bit of personal profit from it. Instead, I'd done nothing and earned jack shit.

'We're good to go,' said one of the suits.

Rosenblum turned towards me. 'OK, Mr Blagden. Please sit down over there by the table.'

I did as I was told, and then the female NeuroStar employee began sticking a set of Neurodes over my head like I was a lab animal. It was all very tense and intrusive, but during the whole setup process, I was grinning inside, thinking: *I've got an ace up my sleeve that you don't know about.*

Once everything was in place, I felt this huge blob moving across the room towards me. It was Bill Goldschmidt, and he came to a halt behind my left shoulder, reading words from a printed page that he held in his hairy fingers.

'You are required to re-upload the missing memory to the NeuroStar Corporation's company hard drive. Once the memory is re-uploaded and replaced, the NeuroStar Corporation retains the right to duplicate and store the resulting file in its company database for an indefinite length of time. The NeuroStar Corporation also retains the right to publish, republish, and use for any commercial purpose, the resulting file including all images and audio that it contains.'

The paper was slapped down on the desk in front of me, along with a pen.

The woman said, 'Could you sign here, at the bottom, please?'

Taking hold of the pen, I scribbled away, almost feeling sorry for the poor bastards.

Picture the scene, dear reader. There I was, sitting there in front of this desk with loads of electrodes protruding from my head. Big, burly Bill Goldschmidt was standing behind me, looking tough and fearsome, his two employees were close-by, twiddling their thumbs, Rosenblum was sat by the wall, looking uncomfortable, and the other officer was trying his best to look stern and tough over by the door. It was at this precise moment, dear reader and valued friend, that I closed my eyes and thought back to my night of passion with the two buxom ladies.

The original video only featured the action in the hotel room, remember, so I didn't have to replay the whole entire night in my head like I did over at Mark Mesmer's. I cut straight to the juicy part.

This was easy to do, of course, because it was all fresh and clear in my mind. The undressing, the ogling, the fondling, the humping away. I visualized it all, in its new HD form, as the officers and executives stood around me in apprehension. Then, in due course, once every curve, every position, every grunt, and every moan had been recalled and transferred through the wires to the NeuroStar Corporation's hard drive, I opened my eyes.

On the screen before me, the most embarrassing sex video you could imagine was playing out. Three fumbling idiots rolled around on a bed, all drunk and incoherent. The movements were sluggish, the words were slurred, and the action was mediocre at best. It was like a pissed-up wrestling match gone wrong.

A horrible silence filled the room—until Goldschmidt growled.

'What the hell is this?'

Putting on my best "innocent, loving puppy dog" expression, I turned to him and said, 'Sorry?'

His face was an angry red balloon that was ready to burst. 'I said, what the hell is this?'

'This is my memory, Mr Goldschmidt. Is something the matter?'

His broad shoulders started to shake and tremble. 'Is something the matter? Is something the bloody matter? Yes! What the hell is this?'

Rosenblum rose from his chair. 'Is there a problem?'

'Yes, there is a problem!' yelled Goldschmidt. 'I don't know what this tripe is, here on the screen, but it's certainly not my video! This asshole here is playing games!'

'I'd appreciate it if you could restrain from using language like that in this police station, Mr Goldschmidt.'

'I'll say whatever I want to say! This asshole over here is playing some kind of game with me!'

The officer by the door stepped closer to the CEO at this point, making his authority known. Rosenblum, for his part, looked down at me.

'What's going on, Mr Blagden?'

'I have no idea, Detective. I was instructed to re-upload my memory of a certain event, and that is exactly what I did.'

'Bullshit!' cried Goldschmidt. 'This isn't your memory of the event! This is something else!'

Looking up at Rosenblum, maintaining unbroken eye contact, I said, 'Detective, I am not lying to you. This is honestly my memory of the event that Mr Goldschmidt of the NeuroStar Corporation requested that I re-upload.'

'Liar!' screamed Goldschmidt. 'You're a goddamn liar!'

'Detective Rosenblum,' I said, once again wearing my puppy dog expression, 'I would be more than willing to take a lie detector test, in order to prove what I am saying.'

I gave myself a pat on the back for this one; it was a cunning move. There was something else working in my favour, as well. I could tell that Rosenblum was unfamiliar with the original sex video, so there was no way for him to know that I was pulling a trick. All of this would've been enough, the tables were turning in my favour, but then, completely out of the blue, Bill Goldschmidt gave me the ultimate helping hand—quite literally.

It happened very fast, too fast for me to fully describe it to you here, but I basically felt this huge wave of muscle and meat fly my way, followed by a tightness around my neck as two strong hands choked me and cut off my air supply. The sound of boots then echoed down the corridor, and the room filled with more personnel. Officers were shouting and yelling over the top of me, trying to prise the disgruntled beast away, and then, just as my vision was becoming blurred and starry, the hairy hands of Bill Goldschmidt lost their grip on me and the CEO was wrestled to the ground.

It couldn't have gone better.

Rosenblum held me to my word. About the lie detector test, I mean. It posed no problem for me, though, because I wasn't actually lying. This, coupled with Bill Goldschmidt's assault, enabled me to walk out of Mapharno City Central Police Station the very next day.

I was a free man.

Excerpt from a newspaper article, printed in The Mapharno Times

Rumours of further violent misconduct involving the CEO of the NeuroStar Corporation, Mr Bill Goldschmidt, have been circulating over the last few days. According to certain commentators, an attack is said to have taken place within a main police station in Mapharno City, instigated by Mr Bill Goldschmidt. The purpose of Mr Goldschmidt's visit to the police station is unknown, as well as the identity of the alleged victim.

Several of our top journalists here at *The Mapharno Times* have contacted the administrative staff of the Mapharno City Police Force, requesting further information on this matter, but so far, nobody has been willing to comment.

This latest rumour is unconfirmed at the time of writing, but even if it is proven to be false, the CEO has a history of violent, predatory behaviour. Very recently, he was involved in a high-profile court case concerning a former employee, who claimed that he was attacked by Mr Goldschmidt in his workplace.

Will this negative press and attention have a damaging effect on Mr Bill Goldschmidt's business empire? It's hard to tell. The value of NeuroStar shares over the last month have...

End of Excerpt

When I met Emily a couple of days later, I had to tell some more white lies. She was understandably curious as to why my phone had been switched off for a while, and why I had failed to meet the day after our last phone call, as I'd promised to do. I blamed it all on a bad gig, and a pissed-up punter stealing my phone. It sounded lame and unbelievable as it was coming out of my mouth, but she didn't question it too much.

It felt great to be with her again, after everything I'd been through. I took her to a fancy Italian restaurant in District 7, and we had a nice time. Pasta, bread, red wine, candles, you name it; it was all very romantic. After it was over, we went to a hotel and made sweet love (my landlady's attitude towards me was still rather cold at this point, so I didn't want to risk taking Emily back to my apartment, for obvious reasons).

Eventually, I managed to patch things up with Meredith, my landlady. I told her that I was fibbing about the missing laptop, then I gave her an edited, highly-diluted version of what actually happened. After I was finished, I made it clear that I lied to her simply because I respect her so much, and I didn't want her valued opinion of me to get tarnished. Flattery gets you everywhere.

As for my work, well...my career was still very alive and kicking at this point. The video was no longer around, but the bookings continued to flow. My new material worked, and I polished it and refined it after each and every gig. Because I'd recently had an encounter with a big corporation—I didn't press charges against Bill Goldschmidt, by the way, in case you were wondering—I started telling the odd corporate-related joke. 'How many corporations does it take to change a lightbulb? Ten. One to change the bulb, and nine to buy it out afterwards, and put it out of business.' I was also reminded of an old joke from way back when, which is kind of related to big business: 'Why did Loreal? Because Max Factor.' Hey, don't look at me like that. It got a laugh back in the day.

Life was good again, and I was lapping it up and asking for seconds. However, as any pessimist will tell you: nothing ever lasts. Every piece of happiness carries within it the seed of its own demise.

Something else was lurking around the next corner.

* * *

Here's how it happened: Emily and I decided to eat out one morning. We were sitting in this breakfast diner, an American-style place with red leather seats and milkshakes on the menu. I was munching down some egg, bacon, and toast, and Emily was drinking tea, tapping and scrolling away on her smartphone. If I remember rightly, she was on DoodoShare, but that's not really relevant.

Anyway, as I was wolfing down this food, I felt Emily suddenly tense up beside me, as though something was bothering her. Her slim body went rigid, and she was staring down towards her screen with an intensity that I didn't like.

Turning to her, I said, 'Are you OK, babe?'

She didn't answer at first. Instead, she continued to look down at her phone, lost in shock.

I nudged her. 'Babe, what is it?'

Slowly, but forcefully, she tilted her head to look at me. 'What the fuck is this?'

It was the first time I'd ever heard Emily swear, so my guard went right up.

'What?'

'Here!' she said, passing me her phone. 'Look! What is this?'

I looked down at the screen, dear reader, down at this stupid app that she was on, and I couldn't believe my eyes. There was this manic buzz, post after post, and it was all about yours truly. Or, to be more accurate, it was all about a sensational new video that I was part of. Scrolling down through this DoodoShare app, I was seeing pictures and thumbnails with my face and body on them, along with two others. Everyone seemed to be sharing it around.

'Press play, then!' scowled Emily. 'Let's have a look, shall we?'

'Emily, I don't think—'

'Press play!' she screamed. 'Let's see what you've been up to!'

People were beginning to stare at this point, leaning over their seats to see what was going on, but I obeyed her command and pressed play.

If it hadn't been for the recent fiasco that I'd been through, I wouldn't have even recognized the video. It was like a sensationalized, juiced-up, borderline caricature version of my original sex video. Everything was exaggerated and augmented somehow, as though the clip had been injected with steroids and put under an intense microscope. It was like the best porn film you could ever imagine, every curve and bulge glorious to the eye, and there I was, the star of the show.

'Care to explain?' hissed Emily.

'I wish I could.'

'What's that supposed to mean?'

'It means...'

I was about to try and explain to her, in my usual edited way, that there'd been a video like this that'd been created way before I met her, and that this one was an artistic rendering of the original, and that she shouldn't hold it against me because it all happened before our relationship began, etc, etc. Before I could even attempt to get myself off the hook, however, it became very apparent that the whole entire diner was staring in my direction, including the staff. Like I said, this new video had exploded all over the internet, across all websites and apps, and it was obvious that everyone in the diner had watched it—and now recognized me.

This was too much for Emily to take.

Customers and waitresses were approaching our booth, asking me for autographs and pictures. Men were patting me on the back and shaking my hand, women were fluttering their eyelashes at me, and at some point during this crazed hysteria, Emily jumped out of her seat and ran out of the restaurant. I didn't chase after her. I knew, instinctively, that this kind of thing would be too much for a posh girl like her to handle.

The diner situation escalated even more after Emily's departure. A mob of crazies gathered around the entrance doors, and it took a couple of police officers to clear them away.

I managed to escape, eventually, and hid in my apartment for the rest of the day. I sent a long message to Emily whilst there, asking for forgiveness. She said she needed time to think.

* * *

I know what you're thinking. You're thinking: where the fuck did this new video come from? Good question. And you're in luck, because I can explain. The origin of the new video soon became common knowledge, due to a bunch of interviews and articles that were published in the main newspapers shortly after its release.

According to an unnamed, anonymous NeuroStar employee, the company was desperate to replace the income stream that was lost when the old video was deleted, and so they held a special staff meeting in order to brainstorm ideas. Almost everyone within the NeuroStar Corporation had seen the original video, and so some bright spark in the meeting had the genius idea of getting everyone to upload their memory of the original video to the main company computer, then the most entertaining version could be selected and uploaded onto the NeuroStar platform for the public to view and share.

This worked, of course, due to the aforementioned fallibility of the human brain. The staff members of the NeuroStar Corporation had warped, distorted memories of the original sex clip, so most of their memory uploads made my bedroom antics appear extremely hyped-up and sensationalized. The resulting second video was then monetized and promoted like crazy, boosted with untold keywords and SEO bullshit.

What lengths would a corporation *not* go to for money, eh?

The whole thing reeks of revenge, too, wouldn't you say? Their chosen method of producing the video, I mean. It seems to me that Goldschmidt decided to fight fire with fire, imitating the dirty trick that I had played on him. I suppose I'll never know for sure.

'Why didn't you try to sue them?' I hear you ask. Again, it's a fair question. They'd made a fake video about me, and physically attacked me by this point. Hhmm, how can I put this? Look, I suppose I didn't want to rock the boat too much; I didn't want to push my luck. I still considered myself lucky for having walked out of the police station that day, with a "No further action" stamp on my file. Moreover, Bill Goldschmidt had the means to hire the best lawyers on the damn planet to defend himself, so what chance would I have had?

In the end, I did the sensible thing: I took it on the chin, and stayed quiet. I may be an idiot, but I'm not a complete idiot.

* * *

Another blow came my way.

The new video clip continued to grow and grow, surpassing the original in terms of views, likes, shares, and ad revenue, and my name became inextricably linked to it.

Emily dumped me by text message.

Can't blame her really, can you? I mean, not really. I couldn't walk down any street at this point without hearing the name "Bouncing Blagden" being shouted from the open windows of passing cars, so it just wouldn't have worked with a girl of such high-quality stock.

I know what you're thinking. You're thinking: there are only a few pages left of this book, and things are looking gloomy for Reed Blagden, so therefore the story must have a sad ending? You're thinking: this diabolical book that I decided to read, *Thanks for the Memory*, is going to end on a dreary note, leaving me all depressed and sympathetic?

Think again, dear reader. Think again.

I'm going to point the finger at you here, for a moment. I'm going to point the finger, and accuse you of being a bit rude. Yes, you heard that correctly. I'm calling you rude. Why? Because throughout this whole entire story, not once have you asked me about my current circumstances. The story I've been describing to you occurred in the past, but what about the present? Where am I now? You don't know, do you? You don't know, because you didn't ask me. And you didn't ask me because you didn't care. That's the way I see it, anyway. That's how it feels.

So, do you want to know? Do you want to know where I've been located this whole entire time? Do you want to know where I've been narrating this story from? Yes? OK, I'll tell you. Right from the start, right from the very first page of this book, I've been telling you this story from the steamy, soapy confines of a Jacuzzi. Yeah, that's right! A Jacuzzi! And guess what? I've not been alone, either. I've been in good company the whole time—*very* good company.

Have you got it yet? Or do I need to spell it out for you? I tell you what, you can say hello to them both.

'Hey, Kat, lean over here a minute, will you? That's it, don't be shy. Now, how about saying hello to the reader?'

'Hello, dear reader. I'm Kat. Nice to meet you.'

'How about you, Melinda? Care to say hello to our valued reader over here?'

'Hello, sweetie. I'm Melinda. I hope you enjoyed the story.'

There you go, dear reader. Sad ending? Depressing ending? I think not. I'm in great company. I'm not lying about the Jacuzzi, either. Back me up, girls. Are we, or are we not, soaking in a hot, steamy, bubbly Jacuzzi right now? Kat?'

'We're in a Jacuzzi, dear reader, and it's grand indeed.'

'Melinda, please confirm to the reader that I'm not lying.'

'We're soaking up bubbles in a nice Jacuzzi, dear reader. I'm having the time of my life.'

Don't start complaining about plot holes in the story, either, or anything like that. You know how I found Kat and Melinda again. Mark Mesmer, remember? He wrote down an address for me, after I recollected it during the hypnosis. So there. Everything's airtight and explainable.

Well, this is the end of the line, I guess. It's been nice having you around, and I hope you can say the same about me. My parting words? Reed Blagden's parting words of wisdom? Look left and right before you cross the road, wear sunscreen, stay away from fried food, and, last but certainly not least, limit your time on social media. It's a demon in disguise; it's ruining the world. Don't say I didn't warn you.

One more thing: if you happen to bump into that phony, arrogant, pretentious asshole who goes by the name of James Flynn, tell him he's a twat from me. No, actually, that's not enough. Swing one at him, give him a bunch of fives. Aim for the throat and groin, the vulnerable parts. Don't feel sorry for the prick, either. He deserves it.

If you're going to feel sorry for anyone, feel sorry for me! As I mentioned before, I'm stuck here within these pages, destined to narrate this mess of a story over and over again every time somebody decides to read this book. Why? Because that nettlesome twat, James Flynn, thought it'd be a good idea to write this story. I'll be retelling this yarn for the rest of eternity, or until the universe implodes, or something. Which I'm quite looking forward to, come to think of it.

Anyway, goodbye.

THE END

Did you enjoy this book? I hope you did. If so, why not grab a microphone and shout about it in the street? Or hijack your local radio station and put out an announcement?

Too much? Okay, I completely understand. But why not leave a review for it instead? It'll help *way* more than you think.

Sign up for James Flynn's mailing list, and receive a free audiobook.

Reading Recommendation

If you enjoyed reading this book, you might also enjoy reading
Half-Human Heroes...

EDITED BY JEREMY FEE

NOT ALL HEROES LOOK THE PART

HALF-HUMAN
HEROES

A FANTASY ANTHOLOGY

Half-Human Heroes is an action-packed fantasy anthology which includes stories with characters considered "half-human" for various reasons, such as being a multi-racial/hybrid species, shorter than the average human, lacking some sense of humanity, being possessed, etc.

Despite the derogatory views of others, these characters still manage to (at least sometimes) act in heroic ways.

Half-Human Heroes is available at all main retailers.

A Bunch of Fives

Free Sample

Ignorance is Bliss

(1st Story from *A Bunch of Fives*)

As the small ferry chugged away from mainland Sài Gòn, Eric buzzed with an immature excitement. He'd done a fair bit of planning and preparation in order to make this trip happen, many months of it, in fact, and now, at last, it was taking place. He was travelling to Cần Giờ Island with a friend, and after a hectic morning navigating through the bustling streets of Sài Gòn they were now on the final leg of the journey, crossing the Soài Rạp River.

They were both sat on a long wooden bench that lined the edge of the noisy vessel, facing inwards towards the cars and mopeds that were parked along the centre strip. Eric's friend, Mack, was roughly the same age as him, shared the same taste in music and beer as he did, and on occasion laughed at the same jokes. But from here, however, the similarities ended. Eric was from the States, whereas Mack was from Australia. And whereas Eric had a jovial, enthusiastic aura about him, Mack had that Australian bluntness that people either loved or hated, coupled with a bag full of personal issues that could've been described as paranoid at best, or psychotic at worst.

It wasn't that Mack was completely void of charm, though; an accusation like that would've been unfair. During the few years that Eric had known him, he'd managed to make people smile and he'd even charmed a few ladies in the park, and it was entirely possible to engage in deep, meaningful conversation with the man. Catch him on the wrong day, though, in the midst of one of his moods, and people would sometimes wonder what institution he was on day release from.

Was Eric foolish for inviting his temperamental friend on this trip? Probably, yes. But that was Eric all over: amiable to the point of being foolish. And besides, he was actually trying to help him. Mack's mood swings had been intensifying as of late, and Eric thought that a little trip like this away from the city might clear his head a bit, albeit if the circumstances were a little unorthodox.

Or...*very* unorthodox.

'Do you really think were gonna find Bigfoot on this island?' scoffed Mack, shifting his weight on the wooden bench to face Eric.

Eric was gazing across the choppy water, over towards the harbour of the island. 'Something is over there. Something.'

Mack sighed, shaking his shaven head. 'You spend too much time on that laptop of yours. Too much time on that interweb.'

'You've seen the video. You've seen it for yourself.'

'Aah, another bloody online video!' cussed Mack. 'They're all the fuckin same. Don't mean a thing.'

'Well, what have we got to lose? If there's nothing over there, at least we'll get a little holiday out of it.'

'Yeah, I suppose,' grunted Mack, shrugging his shoulders.

As one of the most scenic, preserved areas in Vietnam, Cần Giờ was always worth visiting. On any given day, one could be treated to the sight of rare birds fluttering among the tropical trees, crocodiles basking in the shallow lakes, macaque monkeys darting and scrambling along the dirt roads and narrow pathways, and huge fish swimming along the coastline of the sandy beach. This was no conventional wildlife trip, though, not by any means. They weren't travelling to the island to see birds, crocodiles or monkeys, they were travelling there to find a certain hominid species whose very existence was the source of furious online debate. For several years, you see, a video of a bipedal creature had been circulating on the web, and if the rumours were to be believed, the video had been filmed on Cần Giờ Island.

"The Cần Giờ Creature", as it came to be known, traipses through a patch of dense woodland during the short video, and strongly resembles the legendary animal that most people refer to as Bigfoot. Like most video clips of this nature, the filming is extremely shaky throughout and the owner of the material is unknown, giving rise to a large amount of scepticism and doubt, but despite this, the lucid sections of the tape are powerful enough to have convinced many people—Eric included.

The trip was naive, some would say. Others would even call it crazy. But so what? They were a couple of thirty-something males with no strings attached to them, little responsibility hanging over them and plenty of free time. They were embarking on a Bigfoot adventure, like it or lump it.

After the ferry had docked at Cần Giờ, the two of them got on a green bus that took them into the heart of the island. The bus journey was a fast, white-knuckle ride with traditional Vietnamese music ringing out from the driver's dashboard radio. Their spines rattled with every pothole and dip in the road, their rucksacks slid across the leather seats with every turn, and at times they feared for their lives, but they made progress quickly. Before they knew it, they were jumping off the bus at a remote stop, and then trekking across a field of long grass with wooden huts dotted across it.

'Is this where we're pitching up?' asked Mack, his tanned, troubled face dropping slightly as he surveyed the wild grass.

'It certainly is.' Eric now held a map of the island in his hands, a low quality sheet that he'd printed out on someone's computer back in Saigon. 'We're going to have to grease a couple of palms when the locals come along, but we'll be OK.'

'I trust you've done your research and made your phone calls,' smirked Mack, well aware of his friend's diligence. 'Couldn't we have rented out one of those wooden huts, though?'

'Nah. They don't run that kind of service here. It was hard enough trying to convince them to let us pitch up a couple of tents.'

Mack considered this for a moment in his paranoid, over-analytical way. 'What kind of service do they run, then?'

'No service at all, really. What do you think this is, Disneyland? Centre Parks?'

'I was just wondering.'

'They said there's a patch of flat grass over on the west side of the field,' said Eric, pointing over towards the semi-distance. 'Let's get ourselves over there.'

By sunset, they'd successfully erected both of their tents with minimal arguing and bickering, paid off an arrogant, brutish local who clearly hadn't graduated from the school of good manners, and had unpacked the portable gas cooker and a couple of tins of beans.

So far, so good. But the real work would begin tomorrow morning, however, when their search for the Cần Giờ Creature would commence.

* * *

'Will you stop complaining? The mosquitoes weren't that bad,'
sighed Eric. He was sweeping away some low-hanging
branches, trekking through the mangrove forest, listening to
Mack moaning behind him about his night's sleep. 'I heard you
snoring after about ten minutes, so they couldn't have bothered
you that much.'

'That may be so,' gruffed Mack, 'but ten minutes after that
I woke up to find myself being eaten alive.'

'I told you to bring a mosquito net. Anyway, let's stay
focused and cover some ground, shall we?'

They were making their way through the island's thick,
leafy terrain, climbing over lumpy bruguiera tree roots
protruding from the ground and cutting their way through
thorny bushes. Their intended destination was the site of the
infamous Bigfoot video, and Eric had circled the map with felt
pen where he believed it to be.

'How do ya even know that the video was filmed down
here?' asked Mack, treading carefully over the dry, root-ridden
ground.

'Because I've done my homework,' sniffed Eric.

'And what are we going to do if we actually see this thing?'

'Take as many photos of it as we can.'

'For who?'

The midday heat was putting Mack into one of his cynical
moods, and so Eric tried his best to steer things in another
direction.

'For me, for you, and for the advancement of science. But
more importantly, if you get a good shot of it I'll buy you a beer
when we get back to Sài Gòn. How's that?'

'What kind of beer?' Mack whined, swatting a fly away from his face.

'Any beer you want, my friend. And I'll even throw in a bottle of champagne for good measure.'

'I'll remember you said that,' grunted Mack, huffing and puffing in order to keep up with Eric's unrelenting pace.

'And don't forget, you can visit the beach while we're here too,' added Eric. 'You like beaches, don't you?'

'Well, a beach would be better than hacking through these poxy vines.'

Eric ignored the whinging, and kept up the pace. *I knew it was a mistake to bring him.*

On and on they went, marching through the green curtains of the humid forest, following Eric's flimsy map. Their surroundings were dreamlike in their natural, untouched way, and the wildlife that chirped and scurried around them was worthy of a zoologist's wet dream. Dragonflies the size of small birds whizzed about frantically, rats darted in and out of holes in the dry soil, huge termite mounds protruded from the bruguiera tree trunks like black cancerous tumours, and every now and then, if they squinted hard enough in the right direction, a small cluster of macaque monkeys could be seen swinging and climbing across the spindly overhead branches.

When they reached a certain point, Eric stopped and trembled with excitement. 'This is it,' he whispered. 'Just over there. That's where Bigfoot was captured on film.'

Following Eric's line of vision, over towards the other side of a small stream, Mack nodded his agreement. 'Yeah, that kind of looks like it.'

'It totally is, Mack! That's the tree right there! The tree that he walks past.'

'And how do you know it was a man wearing that Bigfoot outfit? It could've been a woman.'

Eric turned and gave Mack an incredulous, stony look. 'Bigfoot outfit? Mack, you've seen the video. Whatever it is, it's not some prankster wearing an outfit. It doesn't even look that hairy, for a start.'

'Alright, whatever. So what now? What do we do now that we're here?'

'We scan the area with our eyes peeled and our cameras ready. And if you see anything, anything at all, snap away.'

'Got it,' muttered Mack, with something resembling a sarcastic grin.

The sarcasm soon turned into irritation, however, as time wore on.

'Let's stop for a drink. I'm fuckin gasping!' scowled Mack, swatting flies away from his face. 'So far we've taken five pictures of macaques, a picture of a parrot, and about half a dozen pictures of meaningless foliage. I'm getting sick of this! I need a break!'

'Sshh! Shut up, will you!' Eric crouched down to a kneeling position. 'There's something over there.'

'Oh, yeah, of course there is! Of course there's something over there. It's another fucking monkey! Let's just sit down for a while. I need to drink some water.'

'No, seriously!' hissed Eric, through his teeth. 'I can really see something over there. Over there between those trees!'

As much as Mack hated to admit it, there did seem to be movement from the leafy shadows up ahead. Strange movement. 'Oh shit, yeah. What *is* that?'

'Well, it's definitely not a monkey.' Snapping a couple of photos, Eric added, 'Look at it. It's standing upright.'

'True. But it's...'

'It's what?'

'Well,' said Mack, squinting at the figure, 'it's definitely not Bigfoot, either.'

Edging closer towards the thing, Eric had no choice but to agree with Mack's observation. The creature standing in front of them was no hairy beast, it was no seven-foot-tall gorilla-like King Kong, it was instead rather...human-like.

It was eating something.

'What's it chewing on?' said Mack, who was now as apprehensive as Eric.

The figure before them was around five feet tall, completely naked with hairless skin, covered in scratches and bruises, and had something furry hanging out of its dripping mouth.

'It's a rat,' said Eric. 'It's eating a rat.'

'It's eating a fucking rat's *head*, that's what it's doing!'

For a few moments the two of them watched on in stunned silence, trying to absorb and process the uncanny scene before them. The more they studied the naked figure, the more it looked like a human being. Its feet and legs were filthy from roaming across the bare soil, its arms were scarred from dragging itself through overgrown brush, and its facial hair had grown into a bushy tangle that obscured the lower half of its face.

But it didn't stop it from eating.

Whether it was enjoying its meal or not, was unclear. Its drooped shoulders and unanimated expression gave nothing away. There was only the *crunch, crunch, crunch* of its jaws against the rat's tiny cranium, the blobs of blood and spittle flecking its beard, and the tailed rodent carcass hanging from its filthy fingers.

'That's a man!' stammered Mack. 'That's a man eating a fucking rat, I'm tellin ya.'

'Don't be ridiculous. We've found Bigfoot.' Eric spoke firmly, almost proudly, but there was a trace of doubt in his voice somewhere.

'That's not Bigfoot. That's a naked human being standing in the woods, chewing on the head of a rat.' Backing off a little, Mack added, 'And you know what? I don't really fancy saying hello. I'm off.'

'Mack! Wait!'

Mack was off on his toes, leaping back through the big green leaves of the jungle, disappearing from sight.

'Wait! Wait a minute! Mack!'

It was no use. Mack was stopping for no one. And so, after taking one last look at the Cần Giờ Creature, Eric rose to his feet and tried to catch up with his friend.

End of Sample

A Bunch of Fives smacks you straight in the face with a mighty handful of powerful fiction. It packs a punch with five hard-hitting stories, all of which will leave you stunned and dizzy in a delirious stupor.

Within these knuckled pages you will find a professional hitman taking on more than he bargained for, a strange creature roaming a Vietnamese island, a nymphomaniac in the midst of a breakdown, a futuristic society obsessed with social media, and much more.

From round one to round five, you will be taken on a disturbing journey that will unnerve you, thrill you, and force you to question your very existence.

A Bunch of Fives should be approached with caution—it's a knockout!

*"Creepy and mystifying, Flynn's weird tales make for a disturbing late-night read"—**Regina's Haunted Library***

*"You will walk away terrified, gobsmacked, and much more!"—**Erica Robyn Reads***

A Bunch of Fives is available at all main retailers. Grab your copy today.

Book Review Channels

The Nerdy Narrative YouTube channel, hosted by Lezlie Smith. Check out her high-quality book reviews @TheNerdyNarrative

The Lit Show with Jeremy Fee. Featuring regular book reviews for horror and fantasy titles. Check out Jeremy's YouTube channel @jeremyfee

Mindy's Book Journey. For quality reviews of horror, fantasy and science fiction titles, check out Mindy's YouTube channel @mindysbookjourney

Media Death Cult YouTube channel. For high-quality and well-informed reviews of science fiction books, check out the channel @MediaDeathCult

Regina's Haunted Library. For quality reviews of horror books and gothic horror books, check out Regina's channel @ReginasHauntedLibrary

Milton Keynes UK
Ingram Content Group UK Ltd.
UKHW020628021023
429777UK00014B/582

9 798215 345283